Running Smack into General Sherman

Stories from North Carolina to London
(And Back Again)

Jeffrey T Kiser-Paradi

Cover Design by Anikó Nagy

Cover Photograph: James Ardrey Crowell
(1862-1924) and company, circa 1920.

To Tibor
(for all the obvious reasons)

CONTENTS

The Feather Yonder   1

Oakling   33

The Stoney Way   45 ✓

August 1903   73 ✓

The Healer   99

The Photograph   107

The Antique Dealer   117

Pigeon Under Glass   141

Transport For London   155

The Queen's Park   169 ✓

Running Smack into General Sherman   191

The Feather Yonder

I

The sand in the abandoned roadbed was rapidly drying where Will had been lazily constructing hoppy toad houses, an undertaking engineered by scooping and packing the damp, white fineness up over his bare feet, then carefully withdrawing them, leaving a free-standing cave-like structure. Sometimes, he would catch a live toad, and with some effort force it into the house, but the frightened amphibian never seemed to appreciate his efforts. Expecting to peer inside and see a contented Mr. Toad, perhaps taking a nap in his nice, cool new home, Will was always left a bit crestfallen when such was not the case.

"Don't let that hoppy toad pee on you," his grandmother would warn. "It'll give you warts. Then we'll have to throw the dish rag under the steps."

His mind raced with the mysterious possibility of this.

"How do you throw it under the steps?" he would ask.

"You just throw it under there, I reckon," she

would answer, forgetting that the only steps he would have ever seen were the modern type, which precluded anything being thrown under them.

The climbing sun was already hot, the sky an incandescent white, the blue having been burned away by the summer heat. When he looked down, the ferocious sun beams would cast themselves, from the back, through the lenses of his glasses, projecting bright, white, concentrated discs on the sand below him. Although it was still relatively early in the day, the cicadas were buzzing, filling the air with their insistent, alien drone. He knew that if you touched the tree on which they were perched, their pulsating buzzing would cease momentarily.

"Now come on and get in the automobile," his grandmother yelled from the back porch.

This morning she was wearing a violet-coloured, Sunday dress, and her large, swollen ankles were clad in black leather, low-healed, dress pumps. On her arm hung her black, patent-leather, Sunday handbag, which he knew to contain nothing more than Kleenex and Wrigley's Double-mint Gum. Her attire meant one thing and one thing only: they were about to go visiting. She was not dressed in her usual clothing, which consisted of a cotton print dress with cotton print apron of a completely divergent pattern tied around her ample waist. Heavy support hose turned down to just above the knee and rubber-soled house slippers in a floral pattern completed her ensemble when at home. The hose could be quickly turned up should company come.

The last of the dew was rapidly evaporating from the grass, but even so, Will's sandy feet became wet. He ambled toward the car through the zinnia patch, a plot planted by his grandmother on the hillside above the road in order to present passers-by, in their vehicles, with an impressive display of colour. The shades were bold, electric, almost vulgar. Pinks, reds, yellows, oranges, and reds were all thrown together, what his grandfather would call a Duke's Mixture. His grandmother planted for spectacular effect, not subtlety.

His grandfather was already sitting in the car, the doors open, one foot placed inside and the other foot resting on the sandy ground. He too had changed from his usual outfit of Osh Gosh overalls, brogans, and broad-brimmed yellow straw hat with inset green celluloid visor, to light summer-weight trousers, check short-sleeve shirt and his dress, summer hat in dark grey straw. The large car was partially shaded by an old, decaying Umbrella tree and was coloured a mixture of oxidised, mint green paint and rust. The elaborate grill, peeling and pitted, was obviously only a shadow of what it must once have been, a panoply of gleaming chrome plate. The old man, grabbing hold of the edge of the windshield for support, slowly drew himself up and pulled open the reluctant backseat door, which groaned loudly like a complaining old, stiff-jointed, farm animal.

Will was greeted by the smell of hot, scorched, decaying leatherette, and the escaping heat hit him like a swarm of perturbed bees. It burned his bare legs as he climbed onto the deep seat, and he could feel it through the back of his shirt.

His grandfather closed the door behind him and eased himself back into the driver's seat, saying to no one in particular, "Hot."

Presently, the form of his grandmother approached, screen door slamming behind her, pausing momentarily to deadhead a bright pink petunia in a planter. After she seated herself, the car haltingly lurched forward and slowly bounced its way down the hill over the driveway – this was little more than a pair of worn tracks in the grass – to the blacktop of the road down below.

"Where are we going?" Will asked.

"Going to the dogs," his grandfather sang.

"What?" he asked.

"We're going to Aunt Sudie's," his grand-mother corrected.

"Where's that?"

"Not far, not even as far as Shuffle Town," she said, referring to the crossroads a few miles away, the main feature of which being a small store advertising, "Live Bait."

"You want to go to Shuffle Town?" his grandfather teased. "We'll take you to Shuffle Town and throw you in the river."

"Nuh uh," Will protested.

He knew his grandfather's humour too well to be taken in by it.

The car accelerated to a speed of around thirty miles per hour, which it kept to, deviating from it only to slow down at an intersection. Even Will knew that this was slow, nothing like the pace at which his father, and especially his mother drove. Therefore, this deliberate, processional conveyance lent a journey with his grandparents a gravity, a heightened significance that was absent when travelling with his parents. One only needed to observe the line of vehicles that always gathered behind the old car in its progress, like a solemn, funereal motorcade, to gain a sense of its moment. There was practically no breeze being stirred up.

He stood up from the deep back seat and placed himself behind the driver's seat, attracted by some movement in the vicinity of his grandfather's hat, directly in front of him. In the satin hat band, was placed at a jaunty angle, a small feather not more than four inches long. It was trembling, dancing practically, in the feeble wind blowing in through the window. He reached up and stroked it, it seemingly dancing around his finger in response. The movements seemed not random to him, but intentional somehow, like there was a pattern, a translation of information to be grasped if only one knew how to read it. For a few moments he was completely engrossed by it, marvelling at the sheer animation of it, until he was distracted by the looming presence of a large, impatient Southern Bell truck following close behind them.

Eventually the car slowed, slower even than its accustomed pace, the steady click of the indicator prefacing a laboured turn into a gently curving, red dirt drive, which left the headlong rumble of the accelerating truck behind on the blacktop. Immediately, Will was presented with the scene of a large, two storey, white clapboard house, partially obscured by large, somewhat deformed oaks, old trees, the sort of trees that display the scars wrought by years of human intervention, their limbs cut and chopped away arbitrarily, for reasons unknown. The house, solidly rectangular, was the sort of structure that everyone would call a farmhouse, although practically no one, if pressed, could define exactly what that meant. Roofed in rusty, vertical sheets of tin, it featured a broad porch running full-length along the front, which was supported by sturdy, unadorned, square columns. The façade, in composed, restful symmetry, consisted of five evenly-spaced sash windows across the breadth of its upper storey and four below, under the porch roof, with the black void of an open door in their centre. A pair of tall, orange brick chimneys, like stalwart sentinels, stood guard on either end. It was all so wonderfully plain, not a superfluous element to be found anywhere in its architecture. If what is to be taken as truth, that ornament is crime, then this was a home that maintained a clean and unblemished record. It was a pile arresting in both its elegance and simplicity.

On top of the grey-painted planks of the porch sat a set of red and white metal tub chairs and matching glider, with white lattice-work cut into each seat and back. The chairs faced the house, their backs to the drive, and were tipped forward, top edges leaning against the clapboards, like worshipers facing their sacred object.

The car came to a stop right at the edge of the porch and let out a rattle and a sigh to indicate the finish of the journey. There before the porch was a huge, flat, river rock, laid out to serve as a step. Snaking through this old bit of stone was clearly visible a vivid, auric vein, reminding all who trod upon it that this part of North Carolina was once gold country. Either side of the stone was bedecked with tall, ungainly Four O'Clocks, the blooms tightly closed, awaiting their appointed hour to open. In the distance, they were greeted with the strange, primitive squawking of Guinea fowl.

An ageing woman appeared at the door, barefoot, wearing Bermuda shorts and a white blouse with the shirt tails out. She waited patiently as his grandparents opened the heavy doors, using them to pull themselves out of the car.

"Hey, hey there," she shouted, producing a toothy grin. "So you did get here?"

"Naw, we're still at home," his grandfather answered, a bit of his typical, gently sardonic humour omnipresent.

She laughed, asking "Is it hot enough for you?"

"Eh law, ain't it awful? It's hotter than blue blazes," his grandmother answered.

"They're calling for it to get up to ninety-five today."

"Oh my law, don't that beat all? My flowers is mot now burnt up.," his grandmother said.

"Hey there boy, " she directed toward Will.

"What's your name? Whose is this one?"

"That's Joan's littlest one," his grandmother said. "Can you say hey to Lucille?"

He stared up at her fancy, black glasses and curled red hair, which was framed by the flaking, beady board porch ceiling high above her, painted "haint" blue. This was his cousin, Lucille.

"Come on in and see Mama," she hollered.

Hers was a voice amplified through years of addressing the aged, the hard of hearing.

"Jason's round here somewhere with the pony. That's all he does nowadays is mess with that dern pony."

"You want to see that pony?" Will's grandmother asked him.

Shaking his head in the negative, he grasped her hand with both of his and buried his head.

"Maybe after a while," she added.

They followed Lucille into a dark, cool hallway, sparsely furnished. Directly ahead, down at the far end of the rectangular room, glared a bright rectangle of another open door, offering a view down a long, sun-baked back porch. Off to the left, they stepped through the door into a sizeable, square room, high-ceilinged and white. The walls were made up of smooth, horizontal planks. Identical planking could be discerned on the ceiling, which seemed to float unfathomably high above.

Opposite the door, stood an ample, old-fashioned, fireplace with painted, wooden mantelpiece, flanked by two closed windows, roller shades pulled halfway down. The mantelpiece consisted of two free-standing pilasters, faintly classical, topped by a deep frieze with a blank, centre tablet, and crowned with a high mantel shelf. It had obviously been crafted by a local artisan ages ago during the construction of the house, a craftsman who had managed, even through his limited resources, to create an assemblage which imparted a grandiosity and spoke in a coherent, classical idiom, albeit an idiom watered down by its removal in time and distance from the source. On the mantel shelf was centred a large, old, wooden clock, which resembled a wide, dark picture frame. It ticked softly, in a manner that gave the impression that it was quietly, methodically murmuring something. Beside the clock was a small, turquoise vase holding a single peacock feather.

He paused, letting his eyes adjust to the dimness, and he noticed the smell of Vicks and something else that he couldn't identify. Looking to the right, he was taken aback by an enormous dark object, which he could not at first distinguish. Only after a second, did he realise just what it was he was standing before, that he was being confronted with an old, imposing wooden bedstead, the scale of which left him dumbfounded. He had never encountered anything such as this before, and he struggled to take it all in. The footboard, the bit nearest him, was equal to his height if not higher. The headboard, made up of rows of horizontal rails and panels, seemed to stretch nearly to the ceiling,.

This was topped by a heavy, rolled cornice adorned with a carved scroll. The wood from which it was fashioned had aged until it was nearly the colour of jet, the variety and grain of the timber completely obscured, as through some agent of ritual, age-old smoke. It commanded a ceremonious presence, cloaked with all the gravity of an old, dark, reredos. Everything in the room seemed to roll away from it and yet gravitate toward it at the same time.

Only secondly did he notice, in the very centre of the bed, making little more than a ripple in a cotton sheet white as an altar cloth, lay a tiny, shrivelled old woman, propped up on some glowing white pillows. She lay motionless, open-eyed and inscrutable as a sphinx. He was frightened by the apparition, an electric-like shock running up and down his body for a second. However, the feeling dissipated within a moment, when she was roused from her suspended, mummy-like state, eyes blinking, this coinciding with a croaking hoarseness issuing from somewhere within her.

"Who is it? Oh land sakes, who all's that come to see me?" she said.

Her wizened face, sagging flesh, was a series of fine, interconnecting lines, like that of an old crazed, jug, no longer white but aged to translucent yellow. Thin, white, wispy hair was pulled back off the face by small, tortoiseshell combs, and perfect white teeth, too large for her shrivelled face, obviously fabricated when she was a younger, larger woman, protruded and parted her thin, colourless lips. The eyes were an opaque, clouded blue, such as a painter would render.

His grandmother and grandfather made their enthusiastic salutations in the direction of the bed, his grandmother sidling up bedside and taking the woman's bony, spotted hand in her own.

"Where'd you get that perty night gown? Aint' that perty?" she sang. "That's mot now too nice to wear."

"I didn't know you all were coming over here to see me," the old woman croaked.

"You did too, mama," shouted her daughter across the bed, "I told you first thing this morning that Uncle Sid and Aunt Florence were coming to see you today."

"Did you? I don't recollect you saying that."

"That's how come I pertied you up."

"Eh lord, my mind's got so that I can't recall nothing, not one thing."

His grandmother pulled up a red, painted, rush-bottomed, straight chair and sat herself down heavily by the bed. This was the cue that everyone else could now, politely leave.

"Uncle Sid, you want a glass of tea?" shouted Lucille. "Come on out to the kitchen and I'll fix you a glass."

This left Will alone with the two sisters. Along with the sharp smell of Vick's, he could also now recognise the scent of old ladies' powder, and an undercurrent of something else his young nose couldn't identify, although his grandmother could easily have told him, as she knew all too well, that it was the permeating odour of decaying flesh. He stood next to the chair, leaning shyly into her.

"And who's this wee piss ant here?" said the old woman pointing to Will.

"That's one of Joan's."

"Joan's? Great day in the morning. Hey there booger."

"Say hey to Aunt Sudie."

He uttered a timid, "Hey."

"Joan's not old enough to have any young'uns is she?"

"She's got two, and this 'un's the baby," insisted his grandmother.

"Law, I didn't know that."

"Good gracious, Laura Jane's already a going through the change."

Will looked up at his grandmother and asked, "Grandmaw, what's the change?"

The old woman let out an amused croak and wheezed, "That's nothing you won't ever have to worry about little banty."

She made the motions of laughing, but no sound came forth from behind the parted teeth.

"Oh Mercy, why don't you go outside and find that boy with that pony," his grandmother said.

He wanted nothing to do with some boy he didn't know, nor any pony for that matter. Neither interested him. He wanted to remain in the cool of the tall room, the telling, mesmerising sound of the clock ticking, and the withered old, white-wrapped, wraith of a woman. Nevertheless, his grandmother was insistent.

"Go on," she said, "Go find that pony."

He reluctantly turned and slowly left the room, noticing the doorknob on the great panelled door, round, lustrous, and white as the full moon, on his way out.

He could hear Lucille with his grandfather out in the kitchen. "How's your corn doing in all this heat?" she was yelling.

The screen door slammed behind him, and he paused on the old, gold-streaked step, as though awaiting direction, wondering how best to avoid any encounter with roisterous boys and horses. Progressing along the Four O'Clocks, he soon approached the end of the porch, and turning the corner he was immediately face to face with one of the house's magnificent chimneys. Wide at the bottom, it gradually narrowed as it ascended the side of the house, in the manner of a huge ceremonial pylon. The crumbling bricks were the colour of the ground upon which they stood, a rich, livid orange, the never-ending, sacrificial work of bees having eroded the mortar until each brick was clearly defined, skeletal, seemingly standing on its own. This massed stack appeared as though it had always, from the beginning of time, stood silently rooted to that very spot. He could not begin to imagine that there had ever been an age when it had not existed, and yet it hinted, from its colour, that it had perhaps grown from this very earth, out of this clay, thus indicating that there was, however remote, a birth of sorts. This could have been, for all Will knew, the site of creation itself.

The Guineas screeched somewhere off in the distance. They emitted a sound of squeaky, slow-turning wheels, like those wheels for prayers, rhythmically spinning.

There was, however, a more immediate utterance catching his attention, that of the low, growling whinny of a horse. Not far off was the pony to which his grandmother was referring. It was a shabby looking Shetland, the colour of a mud-stained sheet. Whether the animal was dirty, tinted with native, Carolina red clay, or that this was its actual colour, was impossible to tell. Hesitantly, Will drew nearer. It was being ridden by a stocky boy, dressed in dirty shorts and tee-shirt, his cousin Jason. He was riding bareback, but with bit and bridle. His sallow skin and complexion seemed to mimic the pale shade of the pony, as though the two had either been in the same place recently or perhaps had come from the same place originally. The soles of his bare feet appeared almost unnaturally orange.

Older than Will, he was in that last stage of childhood, just before the sulky, insolent possession of adolescence takes over. Knowing full well that he was being watched, he initially ignored his cousin who looked on passively. He put the pony through its paces, first this way and then that across the grass, until finally, he directed it toward Will and pulled aggressively on the leather bridle to bring it to a halt, the animal rearing its heavy head back peevishly in response. Will detected something sharp-smelling and vinegary, which he could not decide was from the horse or from his cousin. Either way, he didn't like it.

"What you wearing them glasses for? Can't you see nothing?" Jason asked.

Will shrugged his shoulders and toed the ground.

"You know how to ride a pony?"

Will shook his head.

"Bet you don't even know what a horse is like?"

Will shrugged his shoulders.

"You're scared of him, ain't you?"

He shook his head again, more emphatically.

"Yes you are," his cousin accused, "You're scared."

"No I'm not," Will said.

"I bet you are. I bet you're chicken."

"No I'm not," Will said.

"OK then, if you're not scared, then come over here and pet him on the nose. Go on then. If you're not chicken, come pet him right on the nose. Just one time," Jason said.

Reluctantly, Will stepped forward and held up his hand in the direction of the pony.

"Come on. What you scared of?" his cousin persisted.

Will moved one more step closer, arm outstretched, in order to touch the animal on its broad pulsating, nose. He could feel the hot breath dampening his fingers.

Just as he was about to lay his hand upon it, the animal reared its head back, eyes bulging, opened its immense mouth, revealing its flat, yellow teeth, and bit him square across the knuckles. Will let out a terrified shriek, and he turned and ran back in the direction of the house, the sound of his cousin's laughing following him mockingly through the yard. He climbed the step and ran into the house to his grandmother, hysterical, tears in his eyes.

"What's a matter? What's ailing you?" his grandmother asked, wrapping her arms around him, her voice alarmed.

"That horse...that horse bited me," he managed to get out between his wailing sobs.

"Bit you did he?" the old woman rasped. "That pony's mean as the devil, but then that there Jason is pert near as mean as the pony."

She collapsed into a fit of mirthful coughing. "One of 'em's about as bad as the other'n. I'd say they're about tit for tat, mean as all get out."

"Let me see it," his grandmother said, taking his hand in hers. "Lord, it didn't even break the skin. Bend your fingers. Oh, it's all right. I reckon you'll live. It just scirt you 'uz all."

She enfolded him in her arms and he snuggled at her breast, relishing the cool, loose skin of her mottled, farm wife's arms. She smelled faintly of biscuit dough.

"Hey there," the old woman offered, "I reckon if you juke down right over yonder and pull open that door, there's some candy in there. I have to keep it down there, because if I don't, that Jason is that there hateful, he'll eat it all up."

Timidly, he left the protection of his grandmother's embrace and went to the old-fashioned wash stand that was acting as a bedside table, and retrieved a tin of butter mints.

"Just one of them," his grandmother said, "We're fixing to put dinner on the table afore too long. What do you say?"

He thanked her, and produced a sniffle, just to show that he was still *in extremis* and not to be entirely bought off by a mere butter mint. From the height of the mantel shelf, the old clock rattled into life and began its measured striking, the gong eerie sounding, like an invocation, seeming to recall something remote and distant.

"What's that there on your shirt?" the old woman asked.

Will looked down, then back up at her, with a puzzled look. His cotton knit shirt was striped horizontally, rows of solid red alternating with rows of red dashes, like the ruled lines of a *Fat Boy* tablet.

She directed her bony, crooked finger and raked it along the dashes and said, "Look a there at them horses running across there. You see them horses?"

Again he looked down at the shirt then back up to her, perplexed, his scrutiny intensified by the thick lenses of his glasses. To him, the black of the bed behind her seemed to stretch up forever. She let out a little wheeze of a laugh.

"Look at him just a studying me. What is it you see there boy?"

"I saw Wilhelmina at Circle Meeting," his grandmother interjected.

"What's she allow?" the old woman replied.

"She said the doctor told her that her heart's that bad, that she could drop down dead as a doornail if she didn't get her some rest."

"Shoot fire, she don't do nothing as it is but watch her stories all day long, old no account thing."

At this she wiped her nose with a tissue she had secreted in the sleeve of her gown.

Still holding half a mint in his hand, Will wandered to the other side of the room. Spying a large, old, oak table in the corner, he crept underneath it, hiding himself behind the fringed, white cloth hanging over the edges. He crouched, the large, fat, turned table legs all about him like ancient columns, the fringe like a baldachin. The two old women carried on talking. Thinking he had left the room, the conversation turned to matters more grave.

"Girl, I'm plumb give out," the old woman said.

"I know it,' his grandmother said, "You just need to rest up some more and you'll be feeling fine."

"I'm not going to be fine. I can see it. I'm give out and I'm ready to go home, Florence. I'm ready to go home and see my Robert, and see that sweet little young'un of mine what died so long ago."

The clock ticked steadily, methodically. Entrancing, it whispered like a mystical, gnostic chant. He strained to divine what it could be telling. He longed to know. Perhaps one day, he thought, he would possess the knowledge, like touching the tree trunk to stop the cicada from singing, it would be revealed to him. He wondered if the old woman knew. Did she hear the secret litany the clock was intoning, the old woman with the cloudy eye, the crone who spied the horses in his shirt?

"She won't nothing but a wee thing," she continued, "not six months old, that baby girl of mine, carried off by the fever. I'm ready to go home and see that wee baby, wee baby Zelda. I can see it."

"I never heard tell of anybody talking so crazy," his grandmother said.

"I tell you I can see it. If I was to not wake up tomorrow, if the Lord was to come and take me this very night, come like a thief in the night, a thief in the night, it would not bother me one bit, not one bit."

"You hush up," said his grandmother.

She kicked her swollen leg out, making the chair squeak in the process, as though she were kicking some sense into her sister.

"The only place you're a going to is the crazy house. We're liable to carry you up to Morganton, you keep talking like some simple something. You'll get better a fore long, and then won't you be ashamed of yourself carrying on like all get out?"

She swung her arm in a circular motion, punching the air for emphasis, then clutched it hard to her belly, hand still clenched in a fist. Of course, this was all front. She didn't believe a word of it, but said it as perfunctorily as the small talk that is exchanged with the man who came door to door selling calendars for veterans. Her sister knew this as well, but said nothing. How many times, in her own back bedroom, had his grandmother herself stared at the murky, fading picture on the wall of her own long-dead child and asked how long it would be before they were together again?

After a few moments, she said, "They reckon Adrian's coming down with the sugar diabetes."

II

The slow-moving car, green and rust on the blacktop, was travelling at its measured, cortege speed.

"All this time, she's had my Pyrex dish, ever since the funeral. Look like she could have brought it back over here when she was going up town or somewhere, the way she gallivants around," his grandmother said.

She was looking out the window as she spoke.

"I reckon they've been that busy, fixing up the place," she said. "I've never seen the likes, a doing this and a doing that."

She grasped her hands together into a tight ball and drew them close to her belly for emphasis.

"It's her house now. She can do what she wants to with it," said his grandfather.

"Well it don't hardly seem right, no longer than Sudie's been gone."

"She can burn it down if she takes a notion to," insisted his grandfather.

His grandmother refused to dignify so ridiculous an idea with a response. Will stood behind the driver's seat and watched the feather in his grandfather's hat blowing in the wind, wind given more velocity and concentration by the window being rolled down only a few inches in the crisp autumn air. The sky was a sharp, clear blue, made even more pronounced by the ruddy explosion of colour present on the trees. It reminded one of a photograph, some bucolic scene found on a five hundred piece picture puzzle.

He stroked the feather with his finger, caressing one side bisected by the central spine and then the other. The wind current shook it wildly, animated it as though it were conducting some esoteric ritual, each movement conveying a meaning known only to itself, and well beyond Will's understanding. Like a dishrag thrown under the steps, he could only wonder at its explanation.

Then without warning, as he stroked it, the feather dislodged itself from the hat band, and carried by the wind, launched itself straight out of the window. It happened as quickly as the blinking of an eye. Will stood there, without moving for a moment, trying to comprehend just what had happened. The feather was not on the back seat, nor had it landed on the floorboard. It was gone. He looked over to see if either his grandfather or grandmother had noticed. They had not, so quickly and silently had the feather vanished.

"Christenburys," his grandfather announced, indicating they were passing by a congregation of ramshackle little houses belonging to a local clan.

A grimy, life size, plastic Santa Claus, covered with bird droppings, waved blindly from one of the front yards, something it had done for nearly a year now. His grandfather absent-mindedly drummed a tat too with his open palms on the steering wheel, the Santa grimacing fixedly as they passed. As quietly as he could muster, without attracting notice, Will backed himself away and sat down in the back seat. He stared out the back window, pretending to be engrossed by the large Pepsi truck tailing close behind them, wondering if he could somehow, possibly learn where that feather had blown.

He climbed out of the open door his grandfather was holding open, anxious to leave the car, should the subject of the missing feather suddenly come to fore. Chrysanthemums in rust and orange stood where months before the gangly Four O'clocks had been. As they climbed the old river rock step with its gleaming veining, their ears were accosted, as if in the midst of a swarm of clamouring insects. It was a frantic, enveloping babble, which as they neared the door, revealed itself to be the blare of television commercials escaping from within.

His grandmother pulled open the screen and shouted, "Anybody to home?"

They stood there, expectant, until she repeated, "Anybody to home?"

This time they felt a mild tremor through the old floorboards from somewhere inside, and within a second there appeared Lucille.

"Hey, hey, hey there," she shouted. "Come in the house. My goodness gracious."

"We 'uz about to think the booger man had got you," his grandmother exclaimed.

"Lord, I didn't hear a soul."

"I'm not surprised, all that racket. Sounds like a plague of locusts in there," said his grandfather.

"Good to see you," she laughed. "How are you? Come on in the front room."

His grandfather nudged him toward the room on the left, from where the noise was coming.

"Softens your hands while you do the dishes..."

As he entered, he looked toward the old mantelpiece. Anticipating the dark, the sepulchral quiet, he was instantly struck by a change in the room. Gone was the old picture frame-shaped clock, with its gentle, reassuring ticking. In its place was something else, another clock of sorts, attached to the wall, vaguely starburst shaped, with shiny gold rays pointing outward from the centre, where was situated the small clock face. There, he saw a tiny, red needle looking as though it were cutting in its circumnavigation.

"Carol, show us what's behind door number three."

Expecting to find the huge, blackened bed to the right, with the tiny, shrivelled little shell of a woman placed in it, he was stunned to see that it was no longer there. It was not there, nor was the croaking old crone. It was all gone, as robbed as an empty tomb, as though it had never been there in the first place. In its place, where the bed had once stood, was now a long, large colour television, in a dark wood cabinet, standing on fancy, carved feet, faintly suggesting the old French countryside. On either side of the large, stuttering colour screen were fixed, fake doors, the panels filled with what looked like gold chicken wire. Behind the wire was pleated, red velvet, from which roared the disquietude of the commercials. It seemed mocking in its cacophony, as though it possessed a sense of its own conquest in the room.

"I can see myself. Cleans down to the shine."

Above the television, where before the headboard had once loomed in its magnitude, was hung a picture in a dime store frame, a copy of a lurid painting in purples and oranges. It depicted a waif-like boy, with abnormally large, black eyes and a sad face. He was leaning against a signpost which read, "Paris 20km." Standing next to this child was a cartoonish horse, also with large, black eyes, eyes identical to those of the urchin it stood beside. They both appeared to be crying. Will stood gazing at the spectacle for a full minute, his mouth hanging slightly open, the flashing, restless images of the television screen dancing in the reflection of his glasses.

"Ooh, ain't that perty," his grandmother cooed. "Look a there at that little boy in that picture."

He stared up at her with a puzzled look. "Is that you up there with that horse?" she asked.

He looked at her again, this time his gaze

perhaps more portentous than puzzled.

"Ajax, stronger than dirt."

Without saying a word, he turned and walked out of the room, out of the door and onto the great gold step. He looked neither left nor right, but stood there, pensive and confused, pondering the gold veining. In the distance, was the atavistic squeaking of the Guinea fowl.

Without consciously deciding to do so, he walked in the direction from where the birds seemed to be gathered, just as one finds oneself heading toward the echoing of a faraway, tolling bell. Passing through a small grove of black walnut trees, the fallen fruits black, cracked, shiny, and littering the ground, he found himself standing before the barn. This was a tall, wood-clad structure, weathered to a silver grey, the same colour as the numerous tree trunks that surrounded it. The rusty tin roof blended into the rusty leaves clinging to the surrounding tree branches. It looked to be as old as the house itself, and certainly no less rooted to the ground upon which it stood. The front, the façade Will was facing, featured one large, octagon-shaped doorway in it. This was dark, almost black, and it reminded him of a large, ghostly mouth. Approaching it, he was met with the heady, mixed incense of hay and horse manure.

The light was low inside, but not so dark as to render vision impossible. It was illuminated from above, but without revealing the source, like in an ancient basilica. He was soon aware that he stood in a cavernous space, which somehow seemed higher and more vast than the confines of the exterior of the building would have allowed for. Where he stood was a sort of hall, with a row of stall doors on the right hand side. On the left, a few feet above was an expansive, hay covered loft. This in turn lead to another, similar loft higher up, and then to yet another one even higher, each succeeding loft more light-filled than the last. From where he stood, they climbed upward - how many were they? - until the higher ones were mostly, but not quite, hidden from his view. Heavy, bleached, wooden posts, seemingly sprouting from the ground itself, soared upward to hold the lofts until they too disappeared from view. There was only the sound of wind blowing through the rafters, a soft rustling, that sound akin to the disturbed streaming heard in uncomfortable dreams.

From the last stall, out of a little window beside the closed stall door, popped the head of the pony. It gave Will a quizzical look with its round, bulging eyes, then shook its head up and down in a unsettling, almost knowing way and uttered a low growl of a whinny. This was met with the flapping of wings, dry, slapping remonstrations of unseen, hidden birds disturbed somewhere above. Will visibly started. The pony turned around, trotted in a circle within the stall and then popped its head back out the window, still nodding its head rhythmically.

From far above, high up in the light, he saw something, something moving, falling, slowly, swirlingly. He followed its measured descent, until he was able to make out what it was. It was a small feather. It floated downward, down into the first loft, until it disappeared behind a dark rectangular object, an object which was leaning up against one of the numerous wooden posts.

So dark it could have been mistaken for a black void, it was as far as he could discern, the only thing in the loft, save for some old soap boxes full of rusty junk. He stood, staring at the form, slowly taking in the details. It was tall and flat, a dusty rolled top with a carved scroll. This was the bed, the bed from the house, the bed from the front room, the bed from the old woman. The recognition of it gave him a shock, a sort of electric thrill down his spine, the sort of shock one would receive when discovering a corpse or the lair of a dozing reptile. The light, cut into dusty stripes from above, fell across the dark, brown wood. He climbed up the three thick rungs built into the structure of the barn itself to the loft and stood there, staring at it. It loomed there before him, enigmatic as a tomb, and he strained his head forward as though he was intent on hearing something. However, his solitude was short-lived. Shattering the quiet was a shout. It was Jason.

"Hey, what are you doing up there?" Jason yelled.

Startled, Will turned to see his cousin standing there below in the hall of the barn. The pony, in recognition, let out a low, rumbling whinny, and shook its head up and down.

"What you looking at that old thing for, huh?"

Jason asked as he climbed up to the loft. "That ain't nothing but a rotten old bed."

He reached into an old soap box and pulled out a rusty iron bolt, a piece off of some old, forgotten bit of farm machinery. This he held up, giving it a disdainful scowl, then hurled it, his arm outstretched at a right angle to his body. It hit the bed with a loud crack and ricocheted into the hay, where it disappeared.

"Stop it. Don't do that," Will shouted. Jason let out a derisive laugh.

"What's it bothering you for? It's just an old piece of junk. They carried it out the door just like they carried old Meemaw out. I saw 'em do it. They took her down to the graveyard and stuck her under the mud, and then they brought this old hunk-a-junk down here. My mamma couldn't wait to get rid of it. It don't belong to you anyhow."

He reached over and picked up an old hoe and trotted over to the bed, laughing the entire time. He then struck the headboard with the hoe and scratched it back and forth, leaving angry, white furrows in the dark wood.

"Pow, pow, pow," he screamed.

"Stop that," Will shouted.

Jason laughed loudly, wildly scratching the upper panels of the bed, leaving a pattern of scratches that resembled a sort of infernal, unreadable script. Will ran up to him and grabbed hold of the hoe handle, trying to wrench it from his cousin's hands.

"Stop doing that,' he yelled.

"You can't stop me," Jason laughed. "You ain't nothing but a little old squirt anyhow."

Will pulled on the handle with all of his strength, his cousin drawing back in response, raising the old implement higher and higher, in an attempt to wrest it from Will's reach.

Jason began singing:

It's about time; it's about space.
It's about time to slap your face.

Will was no match Jason's superior strength and agility, but with one great heave, he managed to yank the hoe forward, the hook of the blade catching itself behind the scroll at the top of the headboard. With one more tug, the hoe unbalanced the great bulk of the bed resting against the post, pulling it forward a few inches, and thus causing it to stand up straight as though it had suddenly been animated from within. It hovered, hanging in the air, like someone who just awakened from a deep sleep will oftentimes sit bolt upright. Slowly, however, rather than returning to its resting position against the post, it began to tip forward. Will fell backward on the hay-covered boards and watched, wide-eyed as the heavy headboard, now unstoppable, traversed in an arc toward his cousin. Jason was still jeering and laughing, holding the hoe aloft in a victorious pose.

He continued to sing:

The Batmobile lost a wheel,
And Robin laid an egg.

He, for his part, only became aware of the inevitable after it was already too late to step or even jump out of the way of the great bed's trajectory. As it fell, it gained speed until it toppled over on him, bringing him down as though he were little more than a sack of corn shucks. The entire barn trembled. It seemed the entire earth shook. The pony whinnied loudly in reaction, and tore round the stable in circles, kicking its hind legs out behind it.

Then all was quiet. A huge cloud, white dust and floating bits, like the aftermath of a conjurer's trick in a magic show, wafted silently through the loft. Only after a great tumult is the quiet so unsettling. Jason lay motionless on the floor, only his head left uncovered by the overturned bed. It was as though his body were in process of being slowly consumed, devoured by an immense, old beast, with only his head remaining to be digested.

Tentatively, Will got to his feet and brushed himself off, staring intently at his immobile cousin. The pony, head thrust through the stall window, shook its head up and down maniacally. After what could have been an eternity, although it was only a few seconds, Jason let out a moan. Still, Will remained planted to the spot, not moving. He looked upward, upward to the loft above and then onward to the loft above that, until the lofts receded from his sight entirely. Satisfied that he could see no more, he turned to the ladder and walked away from his cousin and from the bed, Jason continuing to let out the occasional groan as Will climbed down the thick rungs. He walked, not slowly, and yet certainly not quickly, toward the barn door, catching sight of the pony on his way out. The pale horse shook its head up and down, up and down, and let out another low, trembling whinny, as if in response to his passing by, or perhaps in response to something else entirely. It was a sound as eerie as that voiced by a fleeing demon.

"There you are," his grandmother said as he rounded the corner of the front porch.

They were all standing around the step, saying their good-byes.

"We got to get home. Now then, you go on and get in the automobile."

"Where's that Jason?" Lucille shouted.

"I don't know. May be down yonder in the barn," Will said, not looking up.

"Did you see that pony?" his grandmother asked.

"Yes, ma'am," he said.

He climbed up onto the back seat of the car and stared straight ahead. In the distance he could hear the squeak of the Guinea fowl, low and primordial, like a ceaseless, slowly-spinning wheel, a wheel being drawn by a plodding, hell-bound steed, a creature carrying him into a strange, and as of yet unknown world.

Oakling

Although he much preferred the company of the women - their conversation was much more interesting, especially when they spelled out things that they didn't want him to hear - Will had been hastily scuttled out of the kitchen by his mother and told to go outside. The menfolk had already retreated onto the screened-in porch, not so much because of the heat, which was bad enough, but to escape the busy labours of the women in the kitchen, who were washing dishes after the big Sunday dinner. The men knew, by custom, to scoot their chairs out from under the table and make themselves scarce after the meal. Hanging around could make you the target of some withering comments from the women, their telling you to get out from under their feet and such.

Will was five, bespectacled, and in the words of his mother, too big for his britches. She had her hands full trying to get into his head all the things necessary for a boy of his age to know, from not talking to strangers, to looking both ways before crossing the road, to not playing with matches. His grandmother was given to declaring that he was growing like a weed, and his grandfather called him "Taterbug," because he was like something out of the potato patch. He was in to everything coming and going, and thankfully, he would be starting kindergarten in a few weeks. Although he wasn't quite sure what kindergarten was, much less if he was going to like it or not, his mother, perhaps taking into consideration his fecund imagination, had revealed to him the tantalising detail that his teacher was to be named Miss Infinger, the fact of which had captured his attention in no small way. He was incredibly curious to see just what an Infinger looked like.

The image had stuck in his head, and just a few days ago he had cheekily asked his mother, "Is it Miss Infinger or Miss Outfinger?"

His mother told him with a stiff rattle of the newspaper she was reading, that he knew better than to ask such silly questions.

Rather than face the withering rejection of his older sister and older cousins playing on the car port, he sought out the company of his father, uncle, and grandfather on the porch. He stepped through the glass sliding door, the crazy paving feeling cool under his bare feet, feet which had only a few hours before been crammed into his Sunday shoes. There wasn't much air stirring on the porch, but at least the sun was beating down on the front of the house now, rather than out here on the back. The only shade was provided by the house itself, as the lone, spindly pin oak in the back yard, something just recently planted and with a trunk no bigger around than a child's wrist, would not be making its mark for some decades to come. The house was new, and built in the prevailing style of most all houses at the time: brick veneered, low and rectangular in the "ranch style." It sat in what could only be described as a parched, treeless field, which is exactly what it was, having for years been host to crops of cotton, Irish potatoes later on, and most recently a strawberry patch. Despite the fact, however, that for decades it had been working farmland for the family, or perhaps because of it, the plot seemed determinedly resistant to producing a lawn of the desired, showy, verdant grass, instead turning out a variety of brown, stubbly, roadside weeds and the occasional strawberry, which refused to take notice of or succumb to the current situation.

The men were arrayed, each in a lawn chair with green and white plastic webbing. His father was lighting a cigarette, shaking the blackened, half-burned match before tossing it into a little fabric-bottomed ash tray balancing on his leg. His grandfather, dressed in his church clothes minus the tie, jacket, and grey straw hat, was sitting in the fashion favoured by old farmers from the country: his left knee hiked up from the floor, bolstered and held in place by his interlaced fingers fastening around the shin like a barnyard gate latch.

"I declare," Will heard his grandfather saying, "I don't know how much more foolishness people can be expected to tolerate."

This was obviously grown up talk, the kind engaged in by the men, the sort of thing that Will found little interest in. Usually it was about the Braves, or the Tarheels, or sometimes it was about tyres, or transmissions, or things from the news, none of it interesting enough to elicit his attention. He approached his grandfather, leaning over and placing his weight on the dangling, black-shod foot in front of him. His grandfather bounced his leg back playfully in return, pushing Will back upright. It was the sort of game that they had both played many times.

"The problem is these niggers nowadays are just worthless," his grandfather carried on.

"Look at that Detroit," his uncle said, his ample belly nearly preventing him from keeping his right ankle balanced on his left knee, "them niggers carrying on out on the streets and burning everything down...the entire city on fire. It's pure lawlessness, that's all it is."

Will ceased his bouncing on his grandfather's foot in order to better listen to the conversation. Something had caught his attention and he was intrigued.

His father said, "If it was me, I'd have every no good son of a gun shot right between the eyes, every one of them. Those niggers don't have any business acting like that. And why ain't they working anyway? That's what I want to know."

"Too dern lazy to work, that's why," his uncle interjected.

Will was transfixed, listening to everything that was being said. He wasn't allowed to say that particular bad word that the men were using, and hearing it being thrown about so casually was nothing short of thrilling to him.

"And then them Black Panthers get in there and get them all worked up. They got guns, knives, I don't know what all. There's no telling what all they're going to do next," his grandfather said.

Will didn't know what a black panther was, but he imagined something in the jungle, with big snarling teeth, like in *Little Black Sambo*, but much scarier and without the part about the butter.

"You heard about what happened to little Tommy, Sister's boy didn't you?" his father said.

"He was coming down Norwood Drive the other night and a pack of niggers were out standing on the side of the road, and one of them threw a brick right through his windshield. He couldn't stop, what with him being in nigger town and all. He had to drive all the way home with glass all over him. It nearly scared him to death. Can you believe that? It's just a shame and disgrace, that's what it is."

"Eh Lord, you know not," his grandfather exclaimed. "They's somebody going to be killed before it's over with. It needs to put a stop to it right now."

Will had already heard about the brick through the windshield, and he was picturing his teenage cousin, covered in glass, walking in through the back door of his aunt's house, to the horror of everyone present. By this point, he was completely drawn into the men's conversation, their recounting the general wickedness and all around degeneracy of the coloureds. He had already inferred that they were a strange and different sort, and he knew from experience that they generally lived lives in complete separateness to the one he was familiar with, only intruding into his world in the form of old Mitch who used to help his grandfather slaughter the occasional hog, or Gladys who did his grandmother's washing. This was something new to him, and the revelation of it sent a tingle, if not a shiver down his spine. He was drinking it all in.

"And if he would have stopped, they more than likely would have robbed him to boot," his uncle said.

The other two nodded in agreement.

"I blame that there Johnson," his grandfather added. "He's the one that's got them all stirred up, thinking they're the equal of a white man, thinking they don't have to say boo to a goose."

Will knew that this must mean President Johnson, who, according to his cousins, was a very bad man. His cousin Rick had once shown him a little plastic, toy doll modelled to look like the President, with a black suit and a cowboy hat. Someone had placed a noose around the neck, like he was being hanged.

"That's what he needs," his cousin said with a smirk.

His father then started up about someone named Wallace, who Will didn't think he knew. The only Wallace he could think of was a cousin named Jimmy Wallace, but he didn't think it could have been him.

There was a pause in the conversation, when his father said, "Daddy was telling me that there was a white man robbed just the other day in his car when he was stopped at the traffic light down on Beatties Ford, right across from the Water Plant. Nigger walked up to him just like a jay bird and pointed a gun right at him."

Will had been taken to the Charlotte Water Plant where his other grandfather worked. It was a fascinating place with walls full of dials and men in white coats with clipboards, and outdoors there were huge, robotic machines that combed the filth and trash out of the water. He juxtaposed this with the image of a black, bird-like robber sporting an eye mask and flat cap, carrying a black gun.

"They think everything's theirs to take," his uncle added with a tinge of disgust.

Will's imagination was as busy as a Merry Tiller in a patch of new ground. He was cottoning on to the realisation that he had just gained admission into a more grown up world, a world as strange as kindergarten was going to be, a world complex in its distinctions, and although he couldn't comprehend it any more than he understood what an Infinger was, he was canny enough to recognise its presence. The images of the robber, the men throwing the brick through his cousin's windshield, the burning and rioting he had seen on the television, all upturned in his head, he began to sift through all of his experience for a germ of something, anything that he could make use of.

He remembered that he had once been riding in the car with his parents, going uptown, the route of which took you through the rundown neighbourhood where the negro college was located, where he was always told to make sure his car door was locked. He remembered the car being stopped at a traffic light with vehicles streaming by, one after another, filing through the street opposite. One of the cars that passed was a yellow station wagon, and inside this station wagon was a black man riding in the back seat, a man no different than all the dozens of others who were sauntering down the sidewalks and riding in the cars throughout the neighbourhood. Driving the station wagon, however, was a white man. That was all. Will couldn't remember any more than this, and indeed there was nothing more to distinguish it. There was certainly nothing noteworthy about it, and yet it had stuck in his mind.

Perhaps his father had said something at the time, about the fact of a white man driving about with a coloured man in the back seat, a lazy joke, of the type that white folks loved to level against the coloureds; although if he had said such, Will could not recall. Be that as it may, the incident, if one could even call it that, had stayed with him.

His eyes came to rest on the ashtray balancing on his father's leg. It was small, gold, and weighted on the bottom with a sand-filled, check-fabric sack to give it stability, and in the gold dish intended for the ashes, lay the curled, blackened match that his father had used to light his cigarette. It was all that was necessary. It little mattered that his reading of it was as incomplete as his grasp of an Infinger or even an Outfinger.

Overcome with excitement, he grabbed his grandfather's black shoe and blurted out a little too loudly, "You know what?"

He didn't wait for an answer.

"One time, when we were in my daddy's car, and we were going up that road. You know that road, that one we go up when we go uptown?"

He wanted someone to agree with him, to answer him in the affirmative, but no one doing so, he carried on, undaunted.

"We were going up that road, and we saw this station wagon going by, and this man was in the front seat, and he was driving? And in the back seat was this coloured man."

Will was watching his grandfather, to see if there was any reaction. He quickly spun around to check his father. Not seeing any recognition, but not willing to stop now, he continued.

"There was this coloured man in the back seat, and do you know what he was doing?"

He paused momentarily, for dramatic effect, hoping it would work.

"I'll tell you what he was doing. He had a match....that was on fire. It was on fire....and he was holding it right up on that man's head, right on the back, like that with a match."

He held his hand up, with his thumb and forefinger pressed together as if holding a burning match. Very pleased with himself for delivering what he thought was a masterful indictment of the coloured man, Will turned from his father, to his uncle, to his grandfather, to judge their reception.

None of the men, however, said anything; no one even looked at him. It was as if he had said nothing at all, as if he wasn't even in the room. He could feel his cheeks begin to flush and burn with embarrassment. His temples began to throb slightly. He wanted to run away but was too self-conscious to do so.

His uncle piped up, "Was that Horace's new car he was driving this morning at church?"

Sensing that this provided him with a means of escape, Will retreated over to the railing of the porch, hoping not to broadcast his discomfiture. He stretched his arms over the railing and swung his body forward, swinging underneath, as though he would propel himself right through the screen wire if he could. He looked dismally across the parched, brown yard, which was baking in the heat.

Momentarily, from nowhere, a bird, a jay, descended and landed on one of the few branches of the undersized, lone tree, making it shake rhythmically in the process. Not much more than a sapling, it was spare and weedy, having been dug up in the dark woods behind the house and transplanted into the back yard by his father and grandfather. The jay perched there for a bit, motionless. Then with a mechanical turn of its head, it hiked up its tail feathers and shot out from its backside a soupy, purple and white stream, a good bit of the liquid splashing and marking the spindly tree trunk.

"Now then, wonder what it was that made him take the notion all of a sudden?" he heard his grandfather speculate.

Thinking this was said in response to seeing the bird, Will turned to gaze at his grandfather, only to immediately realise that the old man had missed the entire incident. In fact, none of the men had seen it. Turning back again, he just caught the retreating figure of the bird taking flight, fleeing as quickly as it had arrived, leaving only the stain and the trembling tree in the afternoon sun.

The Stoney Way

The orange school bus, all rounded corners like a huge loaf of bread, slowed on its weary trek up the incline of Humpback Mountain Road and stopped at the bottom of a steep, partially washed-out driveway. The fan-shaped sign, emblazoned with STOP and a pair of red, blinking lights swung out from the driver's side of the lumbering vehicle, alerting anyone around that someone was about to disembark. In this instance, it was completely unnecessary, as there was not a soul around anywhere nearby. David stepped off, not turning to see the doors closing behind him and the heavy, tired bus grind into movement and resume its toiling journey up the mountain, carrying the noise of the shouting pupils mixed with the plaintive whine of first gear with it.

He made his way up the drive, which glittered in the afternoon sunlight, the tiny specks of mica – key ingredient of the local terrain - dazzling the eye. To pave this meagre little track, the harsh mountain elements had worked the ancient rock into stones, the stones into gravel, and the gravel into sand, where gleamed the mica like multitudinous stars brilliantly decorating the heavens.

Upward he climbed, to where the stone and grit eventually petered out into some mean, lacklustre grass at the side of the hill where sat a faded, blue and white mobile home, or trailer as everyone around here called it. There was very little to differentiate it from the numerous other trailers to be found all around rural Mitchell County, although this particular example, because of the pitch of the site, appeared rather unsteady, as if it just might roll off the mountainside if it had a mind to, taking a few of the skinny pine trees with it along the way.

On top of its roof were placed eight old truck tires, something intended to prevent the sheet metal from noisily flexing in the severe Appalachian winter wind. Also, as was typical – in order to allow for escape in case of fire - there were two identical doors (one left and one right) punched into the front façade of this metal box of a home. So as to indicate which was the proper front door, there was a low wooden platform, weathered to a silver-grey, built before the door on the right hand side. On that sat a few folding lawn chairs, of the green and white striped webbing variety and a rather decrepit Petunia in a white plastic pot. As for the scene, it wasn't desolate, nor was it run down. It was just what it was: a house trailer, someone's home, sitting on a mountainside. North Carolina is full of them.

It was here, in this trailer, in a little village

known as Altapass, near Spruce Pine, that David
McKinney lived with his father and mother. He was
a shy, quiet youth just turned fifteen, with a shock
of dark hair, which tended to be curly. However,
since the recent advent of the blow dryer, he
managed, by rigorous brushing and blowing each
morning, to keep it straightened. Curls were not
popular. He carried with him a light blue book
satchel, something he was becoming a bit too old
for, and which as a result, the older boys on the
school bus were beginning to tease him about. Be
that as it may, he would not part with the satchel,
as he couldn't imagine how he would manage
without it, providing him as it did with comfort and
security, holding his pencils and pens, his French
textbook, and his folios of classical piano music. The
other boys, the older boys, didn't carry anything as
effete as a book satchel. They carried any
belongings they had in the pockets of their jeans,
and their books, when they deigned to carry any at
all, they cradled inside the crook of their arm,
balancing them carelessly on their hip. David did
not care for any of these boys, and they, when they
weren't bullying him, ignored him completely.

David was bright and loved learning, but
hated school, the local high school, which seemed
to offer in the way of education, a diet heavy with
exposure to loud, aggressive teenage boys, and
little in the way of study of foreign lands and
peoples, his passion. He was hopeless at science
and maths, and Social Studies consisted primarily
of American concerns, which left him cold. The

remaining classes, such as Gym and Shop, were nightmarish forms of torture, the domain of thugs and bullies.

His favourite class, in fact perhaps the only class he liked at all, was French. His teacher, Mrs. Buchanan was, to be honest, rather lacking in any real knowledge of the French language – her pronunciation had a distinctively western North Carolina drawl to it – but at least she made up for such deficiencies with her genuine enthusiasm, which David was copiously infected by. She showered him with praise for his little reports that he would voluntarily bring to class, usually copied from an encyclopaedia, concerning anything French. Having him stand before the bored and indifferent class, she would instruct him to read aloud, in his quiet, timid voice the tidbits he had gleaned about the Champagne Region, Brest chickens, or the fancy head dress of Breton women.

"Now class," she would say, "David has written us a report about, what's it about honey?"

"Sarah Bernhardt."

"He has written us a report on Sarah Bernhardt. Now everybody pay attention. Go on David."

"Sarah Bernhardt was a French actress," he would begin, his voice timid. "She was the most famous actress the world has ever known..."

A few years earlier, he had been enamoured with everything Scottish. The irony of this was that at the time of this infatuation, he didn't even realise that he was of Scots ancestry. He was labouring under the notion, albeit mistaken, that his ancestors were Irish. In the end, it did not matter, for by the time he had discovered his mistake, he had moved on to become a true Francophile. He scoured the local library for anything to do with France, and more specifically that magic, fabled capital, Paris.

He had purchased for fifty cents a book about French cuisine, something the library was de-accessioning, and spent hours studying its photographs depicting serious chefs inspecting lobsters destined for the dining rooms of the SS Normandie and aproned waiters deboning a sole, table side, while well-heeled customers looked on benignly. He had tried, on several occasions, to prepare some of the recipes contained in the book, with limited success. He was daunted, not so much by his lack of cooking skill, which did not amount to much it has to be said, but by the paucity of necessary utensils and ingredients to be found locally. Crystallised violets and copper moulds were thin on the ground in Mitchell County.

All these interests paled, however, when compared to his real, his true obsession: he had been studying piano for a few years now. Of course, his approach was quite unlike that of a typical adolescent. As with all things he took on, he conducted his piano studies with the intensity and zeal of a Jesuit promulgator. In addition to the required practice, to which he dedicated long hours, he endeavoured to learn everything possible about classical composers and pianists, and in doing so, he had struck upon what he believed to be his destiny. Using none other than the world renowned Van Cliburn as role model, he had decided, a little over a year ago, that he was going to be a concert pianist. Undaunted by the fact that Mr. Cliburn had begun his studies at a much younger age and had been taught by one, whose own teacher had been taught by Franz Liszt himself, he was determined to realise his plans. But, unlike Van Cliburn, who had attended the Julliard School in New York, he intended, when he was old enough, to study at the world renowned Sorbonne in Paris. He enthusiastically looked to what he foresaw as an august future, even though it was obviously apparent, at present, that his designs far outstripped his actual proficiency. His view concerning this was that, far from being insur-mountable, his immediate, and what he saw as temporary, lack of skill was a mere inconvenience, something to be overcome by diligence. He didn't let it disturb his reverie.

As part of this ongoing development of a burgeoning pianist, he thought it vital to keep up with the activities of Lili Kraus, the well-known, semi-retired pianist who kept a holiday home nearby in the vicinity of Burnsville. While she certainly was not the most noteworthy pianist to have ever practised the art, she was indisputably the chief, indeed the only one, residing in the North Carolina mountains. David had seen her play several times at her local benefit recitals, and had even once, after a performance, met her briefly. He was completely mesmerised by her sheer exoticism, by the heavy, brocade gowns that she wore for her performances, objects more at home in a Budapest concert hall than the mundane church halls of Yancey County. It was said she carefully wrapped the hems around her feet while playing so as not to divulge the secrets of her pedalling technique. He was transfixed by her thick, Hungarian accent, when she announced to the audience that she still performed, 'By the Grrrrrace of God." She was gracious and polite when they met, but the painfully quiet youth, who in his appearance and speech, was so obviously a product of the poor, native population (when she asked him where he was from, he told her Alley-Pais, local dialect for Altapass) failed to make a lasting impression on the great woman.

For his own instruction, he relied on a resident of the picturesque village of Little Switzerland several miles away. Her name was Eve Lynn Zimmerman, a local woman who had studied piano performance at the Woman's College of the University of North Carolina down in Greensboro. While she was no Lily Kraus, her solid background was more than sufficient for the fledgling pianist, and she took him seriously, offering encourage-ment for his Parisian plans. Like the French teacher, she doted on him, but also, more importantly, she grounded him, steering him to mastery of the basics before moving on to the flights of fancy he preferred.

"Now darling, you don't need to worry about those arpeggios just yet," she would urge.

"There's plenty of time for that. Now let's count, one and a two, three and four..."

Fortunately, he did display a real proficiency in playing, and this, mixed with his undeniable fervour, made the possibility of his becoming a competent, even a virtuoso pianist, entirely plausible. However, there was one impediment that stood in his way, and this was a very tangible obstacle to be sure. Even though David had been studying piano for some time, his family did not actually own a piano themselves. In order to practice, he had been travelling to his aunt's house after school, playing on her ancient, battered upright. No one in her household had ever played this black, forlorn instrument, and the only reason it was in the house at all is that it had been acquired to settle an old gambling debt years before. He had unlimited access to this piano, it is true, and toiled at it studiously, but the necessity of travelling the four miles each time he wanted to practice was wearing thin, both on him and his parents, who had to chauffeur him, sometimes there and then back again.

It was high time he had a piano of his own. Of course his aunt would only have been too happy to give him hers and finally be rid of it, but he refused this full stop. This was not the instrument for a serious musician. Even his parents saw that. The tone it produced sounded uncannily like that emanating from the saloon in the weekly episodes of *Gunsmoke* on television. However, their endeavours at finding a piano had amounted to nothing more than a disastrous visit to a carpeted, fluorescent-lighted showroom where were displayed in banal, dismal replication, like insects pinned to a board, small, cheap, spinet pianos with strange, foreign-sounding names. These were rejected out of hand by David. Even the battered piece of junk he was playing now sounded better than these little boxes, with their plastic keys and tiny, toy-like sonority.

He had his sights set on something higher, and much better, not some old beat up piece of junk or a new, plasticised, silly thing from goodness knows where. What he wanted was a proper piano, something befitting what he saw himself becoming, a concert pianist. He wanted the kind of piano that he had seen on television, with Vladimir Horowitz seated at the keyboard. What he wanted was a Steinway. He was convinced that this was the piano for him. He had learned that these choice instruments were the best available, being made by hand in Brooklyn, New York, and were the favourites of all serious pianists.

What he was less aware of, of course, was their price. Having written for information, he had received in the mail a Steinway brochure from a piano dealership in nearby Johnson City. He pored over the catalogue for days, like a biblical scholar, reading and rereading the descriptions of the various models, largely neglecting the separate price list the dealer had included. His favourite was the Music Room Grand, but he received a bit of a shock when he placed the yard stick on the floor of the trailer and saw that this hefty beast was essentially the size of the family living room. Of course, the idea was that his piano would reside in his room, which was tiny. The living room was already full, and besides, how could you watch the television with piano playing going on? Even the diminutive Baby Grand was way too large.

Eventually, after much thought, he came to the conclusion that he would have to make do with an upright, and so he chose the Model 1098 Studio Upright, a fitting compromise he mused. He congratulated himself on what he perceived as his level headedness and maturity in coming to his choice of instrument, imagining the praise with which his mother would shower him, when she saw how sensible he had been. So, it was with a real sense of accomplishment that he solemnly handed the catalogue to her, accompanied by his page by page commentary and explanation, with the intended culmination of the desired Model 1098. His mother patiently sat through his presentation, periodically fanning away her cigarette smoke with her hand, listening to the pros and cons of each model. Then, when he had finished, she flipped back through the glossy pages until she came across the price list, a serious frown steadily forming across her face.

♪ After scrutinising the printed prices, she curtly handed the catalogue back to him, saying, "Son, are you cockeyed crazy? We can't afford no Steinway pianer. What do you think we're made out of? Have you seen what these h'yer cost?"

Then, adding for good measure, she exclaimed, "You may as well forget that thing right now.".

This utterly crushed him. He was dumb-struck, tears starting to form in his eyes.

"And don't you go primping up and crying neither," she said.

His dreams of the ultimate pianistic ex-perience were shattered, dead in the water, water the body of which could have been made up of the tears he shed, alone, in his room. He moped around for days afterwards and couldn't bring himself to look at the catalogue for several weeks. /

He stood there in the driveway alone, the drone of the school bus fading until it was eventually lost in the whistle of the mountain wind. There were no vehicles parked in the drive, as his parents were still at work. Climbing the wooden steps, he wiped the grit from his feet at the mat and pulled open the trailer door, which was unlocked. It was rarely, if ever locked. Inside, it was dark and smelled of cooking and cigarettes, unfiltered Lucky Strikes from his father and Salem Menthol Longs from his more image-conscious mother. Dark, sullen, wood panelling clad the walls, and a deep-pile, burnt orange carpeting covered the floor like a mouldy growth. At the small windows hung stale, slightly yellowed curtains, which sported ruffles and tie-backs, reminding you somewhat of a café or perhaps a doll's house. To the right, in the kitchen, stood a dinette set with vinyl-clad, tubular steel chairs and a Formica-topped table in an imitation wood pattern. An oversized, dark oak sofa and matching chair with rust, brown, and orange plaid cushions huddled together, dominating the living area, keeping company with the television set, a wooden, early American, cabinet model standing on four splayed legs.

He didn't stop here but carried on, on past a large picture in an oak frame. It was a print, the surface unconvincingly textured to imitate the brush strokes of an oil painting, depicting a quaint, picturesque, village blacksmith shop under a spreading tree, with the smith engaged in changing the shoe of a lively black horse. He continued down the tiny, claustrophobic hallway into his bedroom, where he flipped on the light switch. Instantly, a large - especially for this small, low-ceilinged room - crystal chandelier lit up, throwing bright, disconcerting, prismatic shapes onto the light blue, chenille bedspread covering his bed and his many pictures torn from magazines adorning the brown walls. The bare bulbs of the light made it necessary to squint in the sudden brilliance. There were photographs of Paris, a picture of Van Cliburn, one of Beethoven, and another of Edith Piaf.

Constructed of a gold-painted, faintly tree-limb-shaped frame hung with tear drop, glass pendants, the chandelier was his prized possession. He had seen it in the Sears catalogue a few years back and had kept at his mother until she finally ordered it for his birthday. Never occurring to him for a moment that a chandelier was an odd thing for a boy to desire, much less to have in his room, he considered it the height of elegance, just the thing one would encounter in a smart Parisian *appartement*.

He put down his book satchel and wearily sat on the edge of the bed. Edith Piaf, as if by design, peered rapturously upwards from her photograph in the direction of the chandelier, as though she had been thrown into a state of ecstasy by its luminosity. What a day this had turned out to be. Not only was it long, endless in fact, but one of sharp humiliation as well. Why, he asked himself, had he gone and done what he had? Why had he gone and told that to his Home Room teacher, Mrs. Newell? He repeated the whole thing in his head, drawing out the torturous details, replaying each one in his consciousness, reliving the embarrassment, until he practically made himself ill. Beethoven glared at him disapprovingly from the wall. /

However, even while he endured the self-flagellation, he knew, knew good and well, that he could not have helped telling it. He just couldn't help it, not today at any rate. Today of all days he could not help himself. He was beside himself, too excited, but excited or not, the degradation of the incident had dampened his mood terribly. He didn't even like Mrs. Newell, his teacher, in the first place, and he certainly was no stranger to her particular brand of cruelty. To make matters worse, he couldn't help but remind himself, over and over, that he really should have known better. Oh, she was nice enough, so it seemed, and full of questions, smiling at you with her round face and button nose, her plaid pants suits that she always bragged about coming from Asheville, but you always found yourself, when engaged in her prodding, her questioning, inevitably being dragged down a road, a stoney way, the end of which left you feeling somehow ashamed of who you were, a bit foolish, and somehow not quite worth what she was.

Even though she had grown up in Spruce Pine and had gone to school with David's mother, she always acted like she was better than everyone else, just because she lived in a split-level house over in Marion. Her husband, Earl Newell, was regional manager for a big furniture company and drove a company car, an Oldsmobile 88. Even so, David's mother, well familiar with the teacher's airs, was ever quick to point out that Mrs. Newell's father had been none other than Vance Nanny, a notorious, local bootlegger, who had more than once spent time in prison and had been known to, on occasion, beat his wife. You certainly wouldn't guess any of this to look at her now, standing majestically before the class, rings on her fingers, frosted lipstick, hair teased high.

Sometimes, when it suited her, she would ask him, her voice with a saccharine edge, "David, is Anita still working down at the knitting mill?"

He would always report this back to his mother, who after taking a long draw on her Salem, and tossing her high, blonde hairdo back, would reply, "Ask her if old Vance is still watering down his liquor. Ask her that. Don't know who she thinks she is. When we was growing up, she only had two dresses and one of them had ink spilled all down the front of it. Ask her if she remembers that dress with the ink down the front of it. Bet that'll shut her up."

While David's father, who was born and raised in Altapass, was completely oblivious to the barbs of Mrs. Newell – she could have lived in Biltmore House and lit her cigarettes with ten dollar bills for all he knew – it was his mother who saw them for what they were and was especially sensitive to their sting. She was not willing to be looked down on by the stuck up daughter of a bootlegger. Thus, it was she who, when David's father once remarked about a change of procedures at the mill due to its effect on the environment, was quick to correct his local – and very telling – plebeian, pronunciation.

"Connelly," she exhorted, "Don't say en-var-rament; say en-vi-rament."

He may have been from Altapass, but that didn't mean, according to David's mother, that he had to sound like he came from Altapass.

David had been on the receiving end of Mrs. Newell's cutting attentions before. Several months earlier, he had announced to her, and to the class, that he was going to Paris. Of course, he had meant this as a kind of statement of his intention, that he was going to Paris, just as he was going to study at the Sorbonne, and was going to be a concert pianist, all, at least in his mind, certainties. He thought that this alone, the sincere declaration of his future plans, would be enough to impress the class and more importantly, the uppity teacher. However, he misjudged Mrs. Newell's cynicism and cruelty. She was fully aware of his dreamy aspirations – they were a source of mild irritation for her – but chose, once he had spoken, to take him literally, at his word, that he was going to Paris and going in the immediate future. Knowing full well that there was little chance of his travelling to Raleigh, much less Paris, she pounced on the frivolity of it like a cat on a canary.

"Paris, really," she said, "My goodness gracious, now that's something else. So when are you going? Now do you have your hotel reservations yet? What airline are you flying on? Are you going to fly out of Asheville to New York, or are you going to drive down to Charlotte? No, I bet you're going to have to fly through Atlanta aren't you?"

Obviously, David couldn't answer any of these enquiries. He had never even been on an aeroplane before. Weakly, he tried saying that he wasn't going just right now, which only gave Mrs. Newell more purchase. Her voice turned from mock sweet to mocking,

"Oh, so just when are you going, Mr. world traveller?"

She then laughed, the class joining in with her, "I don't think I'd pack my bags just yet."

She then laughed again, adding, "I don't think I'll get the glasses out any time soon for that bottle of champagne you're going to bring me back from Paris. No siree, that's for sure."

Today's incident was even worse, far exceeding his earlier drubbing. Home room was basically a segment of the day devoted to taking roll and not much else, in reality a construct to prevent all the students from going to lunch at the same time and thus overwhelming the cafeteria. Mrs. Newell, after reading various announcements, in order to fill in the void of time remaining, had asked if anybody had anything exciting or news-worthy to tell to the class. This was a sort of adolescent version of Show and Tell, which on the face of it, looked quite inviting. More times than not, when no one offered up anything, Mrs. Newell enthused over the fancy dinner she had been to in Morganton, hosted by Earl's company or the shopping trip she had been on down to Gaffney, South Carolina, with women from the church. However, if one of the students did share something, the entire affair could take on a more sinister note. The more clever of the class had slowly come to realise that this could be a minefield, an invitation to become a participant in Mrs. Newell's pastime of ritual humiliation via the subtle, or blunt, put down. It felt faintly like a game of cat and mouse.

"So," she asked, "does anybody have anything they want to share with the class?"

She was sitting behind her desk; there was certainly no reason to stand up for something as insignificant as Home Room and this lot of backward yokels. No one said anything, everyone eyeing everyone else. Then, a plump, simple girl named Claudette Carpenter raised her hand.

"Claudette," Mrs. Newell chirped, feigning interest, "what do you have to share with us?"

Claudette beamed, announcing that her sister Charlene and Charlene's husband Daryl, had just driven down to Myrtle Beach where they had been staying at a motel with a big swimming pool.

"Really," Mrs. Newell said, tipping her round face to one side, and inserting a pointed pink fingernail into her stiff teased hair for a gentle scratch, "What's the name of the motel they're staying at Claudette?"

David shuddered slightly and squirmed in his seat. He sensed where this was going.

"Uh, it's called Ralph and Nadine's Ocean Vue Lodge," Claudette said.

Mrs. Newell wrinkled her nose and pursed her lips.

"Ralph and Nadine's Ocean Vue Lodge," she repeated, "I've never heard of THAT motel."

She then laughed and added, "Sounds like that's down on the highway, over on Seventeen. Do you know if it's over on the highway, Claudette?"

"Uh, I don't know," said the hapless Claudette.

"Hmm, it sure sounds like the kind of cheap motel you would get down on Seventeen," she smirked. "I guess not everybody can stay some place nice, you know some place on the ocean front and with air conditioning and all the amenities, can they honey? Now, my husband Earl and I, when we go to Myrtle Beach, we stay right there on the water – the last time we went down there we stayed at the Landmark; Earl's company was having their convention there – but I don't think your sister and brother-in-law could be staying some place like that. But wherever it is they ended up, I'm sure they are really enjoying it. You reckon they even can get to the water from where they are?"

Then, glancing over toward the open door, having become bored with the subject, and the object of her torment, she added, "Poor old pitiful things, they probably don't know any difference."

Claudette coloured visibly and looked down at her desk. She was not certain what had just taken place, but even she, with her limited intellect, knew that something had, something not very nice. It had never occurred to her to ask whether the motel was on the water, or on the highway, or on the moon for that matter. It had never occurred to her to ask anything, only to be happy for her sister, for whom a vacation at the beach, whatever the class of accommodation, was a rare occurrence.

David knew exactly how the pitiful Claudette was feeling at that moment. He had been there before. He so wanted to do something, he didn't know what, to that smarty Mrs. Newell. He wanted to, just one time, to put her in her place, to wipe that smirk off her face, but there was something else roiling up inside him as well. Combined with his growing, simmering outrage was something equally strong and powerfully insistent. He really, really had something he wanted to say, to tell, and he was ready to burst, practically possessed by his need to tell it. This, mixed with his desire to strike out at the hectoring teacher created something heady and unstoppable.

"So, who else? Does anyone else have anything interesting to tell us?"

Before he even had time to think better about what he was doing, he raised his hand. He felt the blood pulsing in his temples. Mrs. Newell looked over, the ends of her mouth turning up ever so slightly as she did so.

"David?" she said in his direction.

The class all turned to stare at him.

"I'm getting a brand-new piano," he said, attempting to control his breath.

"I'm getting a brand-new Steinway Model 1098 Studio Upright piano, in black."

The class looked blankly at him, some of them having experienced his unasked-for French class reports. As far as they were concerned, he was speaking Greek, or even Esperanto. Mrs. Newell, however, was a different story.

"Do what?" she said, suddenly interested.

She was like the dozing cat, who seemingly lost in slumber, perks up in a flash when it detects the presence of a pigeon.

"I'm getting a Steinway model 1098 Studio Upright piano, in black," he repeated, a bit more thinly than before.

While she was no expert, Mrs. Newell had watched enough television to know that Steinway was a brand of piano, and a very expensive brand of piano at that. She could vaguely recall seeing that name, Steinway, neatly lettered in gold on the side of a huge, grand piano being played by some somebody famous, somebody she couldn't remember the name of, playing something she didn't know the name of. Was it on *Ed Sullivan*? This nonplussed her. How dare this little so and so from Altapass put something before her, indeed try to show her up, with something that she didn't really know anything about.

She was momentarily stymied, uncertain of how to puncture it, to deflate it. She splayed the fingers on her hand, peering at her nails.

"Steinway? Humph. Are you sure about that?" she prodded.

"What happened?" she continued, "Did your mama and daddy get a promotion over 't mill? Matter of fact, maybe they bought the mill. Is that what happened?"

This was cruel, designed to point out, to let him know, that she knew exactly just who he was and what he came from. Perhaps he was still carried by the heat of the moment, but he didn't react, and unfortunately for her purposes, it didn't prompt a reaction from the class. They only took notice, maybe the only time they took notice of anything, when someone was being taken down a few notches, and their jeering was always useful.

She would need to try something else, another tack, and it came to her immediately; it was perfect, and she pounced.

"And is Liberace coming over to play this

Steinway piano with you before you two swan off to Paris for frog legs and Champagne?" she said.

At this, the class erupted into laughter, her swipe hitting its target.

Then, on a roll, tapping her long, pink nail on her desk for emphasis, she delivered her fatal blow, saying, "I reckon you're getting a Steinway piano just like you're going off to Paris to study. That's what I reckon. Lordy bless! What are you going to come up with next? Maybe you and Liberace are going up to the moon with the next Apollo mission, hmm?"

At this she laughed a bit too loudly (a laugh more befitting a bootlegger's daughter than a school teacher) looking about the class, inviting them to join in her kill. David could feel the heat travelling up his neck and into his face. Staring blankly at his book satchel resting on the desktop in front of him, he was desperate not to let this be happening again, this bloodbath.

He stammered, as loudly as he could muster, his voice trembling, "I AM getting a Steinway piano. I sent away for the catalogue, and me and my mama and daddy went over to Johnson City and saw it, and we bought it, and it's coming...."

Before he could finish, the cacophonous ringing of the bell, the merciful end to his pummelling, cut him off.

Presently, he heard the unmistakable sound of his mother's Dodge pull up in the drive, crunching stone in its way under the tyres, and then within a minute, the trailer door open and shut. He dreaded telling her about the incident at school. He dreaded the inevitable outburst from her, the telling off he would receive, the lecture about telling "our business to that jumped-up Miss High and Mighty." She was standing before the sink, staring distractedly at the dishes in the drainer, smoking her cigarette, when he slowly made his way through the dark of the trailer.

"Hello Son," she said, turning to greet him. "How was school today? I bet you couldn't wait to get home could you?"

He didn't answer, but looked down at the shag carpeting.

Her expression changing, she asked, "What? What's wrong? What's happened?"

It was not as though he was especially difficult to read.

He paused a second, biting his lip, then said, "Today at school, I told Mrs. Newell..."

"What? What did you go an tell her?" She put her hand on her hip.

"I told her...that I was getting a Steinway."

"You told her what?"

Faltering, he continued, "She asked in home room if anybody had anything exciting to share, and I told her I was getting my new Steinway, and she, and she didn't believe me. Not just that, she laughed, and she made fun of me."

His mother's face changed, the plucked eyebrows turning down severely in the centre of her face. Her anger palatable, she took a long draw on her cigarette, eventually shooting the smoke out of her tightly pursed mouth in a jet. Then, spinning around, she stomped over to the sink and gave the cigarette a savage tap with her index finger, sending the ash flying. She whirled back around and caught him in her brutal gaze. He waited for her to say something. No doubt there was going to be plenty, and he prepared himself for the onslaught.

"Son, how long-headed are you?" she began.

Before she could well and truly erupt, however, she was interrupted by a loud, high-pitched whining coming from outside, not unlike the sound of some animal in pain. They both turned toward the noise, which grew louder and more recognisable, until it could be, without a doubt, identified as the sound of a heavy vehicle, complaining of the steep pitch, slowly climbing its way up the stone of the driveway. David, followed closely by his mother, ran and threw open the door to reveal the sight of a large moving van inching, a bit hesitantly, toward the trailer. On its side were large black letters reading: *Rankin's Music, Johnson City, Tennessee, "Making Beautiful Music Since 1927."* The setting sun made the driveway appear to dance, the mica sparkling busily.

Perhaps a little too excitedly for a fifteen-year-old, he shouted, "It's here!"

As they both stepped outside onto the wooden decking, the van slowed until it finally decided to stop, and a large, perplexed looking man, carrying a clipboard, lowered himself out of the passenger side of the cab and lumbered towards them. He had dark, greasy hair combed over a bald patch, and his beer gut pressed tightly on the front of his brown work overalls.

"Excuse me," he asked, nodding toward the heavens like someone performing a kind of stage pantomime, "is this Box 164 Humpback Mountain Road?"

His mother, catching the subtle, loaded incredulity of the man's question, that this could not possibly be the address, was nonplussed.

With one arm crossed under her breast and the other propped vertically on top of it, so that her cigarette was in close proximity to her mouth, she said with more than a little sarcasm, "Yes it is; this is Box 164 Humpback Mountain Road."

The man scratched his head and said, "Well uh, we've got a delivery of a pianer for this address."

"And we're expecting a delivery of a piano at this address," she threw back at him (she no longer said "pianer" ever since their visit to Johnson City).

"I believe you ought to have fer us a Steinway Model 108 Studio Upright on the back of that van there," she added.

"Model 1098," David corrected.

"Model 1098."

The man's expression changed from confusion to something akin to surprise. He reached into the breast pocket of his overall and pulled out a pack of Camels.

"Well I declare," he said, tapping the pack to

draw out a cigarette, "I don't believe we ever took a Steinway in a trailer before."

At this he placed the cigarette loosely between his lips and began fumbling for his matches.

His mother drew her own cigarette to her lips and seriously inhaled. Then smiling wickedly, she opened her mouth and broke into a protracted, silent laughter, the smoke shooting out in little staccato puffs in the direction of the delivery man.

"Well hell man," she retorted, "I bet they's lots of things you ain't never done before."

She flipped her ash for emphasis.

"You might not believe it," she said. "They might not nobody believe it. But you can believe this, you 'ins is going to have put a Steinway piano in a trailer by the time you 'ins leave h'yere today. And that's the gospel truth."

At this, she turned to David, her eyes sparkling with merriment, filled with affection and said, "Ain't that right Son?"

Only the mindless, inane shouting of the adolescents could compete with the rhythmic rattling of the frost-covered windows of the school bus, overlaid with the lethargic bawling of the transmission protesting its way to the school. David sat on one of the hard, brown seats alone. All about him, the walls and ceiling were painted the blue-green colour of bread mould. Here and there, where the smelly leatherette covering the seats was torn, odd looking, wiry-black stuffing poked out.

He sat in one of the nondescript seats, neither near the front nor in the back, that is, in school bus hierarchy, nowhere. He rested his book satchel in his lap, his arms securing it to his body, and looked abstractedly out the window, paying no attention to the din all about him.

Momentarily, he lifted up the satchel and raised the front flap and putting his hand down in the pocket, pulled out a small paper-like bit of card, about four inches square, which revealed itself to be a photograph. It was black and white, a bit blurry, with a white border all round it, something from an instant camera. A Christmas present from his father a few years ago, his mother owned a Polaroid "Instamatic," something the manufacturers racily named "The Swinger." Although the quality of the pictures was not the greatest - you had to wipe them down with a little vinegar-reeking sponge in order to keep them from fading into oblivion - they were nevertheless instantly available and ready to see, a marvel.

This is what he held, a Polaroid snapshot, taken last evening by his mother. He studied it in the morning light, just able to make out the image of himself, smiling, standing next to a gleaming, black, upright piano. The glare of a chandelier made an odd, eerie, white blotch in the top left hand corner of the composition, lending the picture an almost ethereal glow. The chandelier bulbs clashing with the flash nearly – but not quite – succeeded in obscuring from visibility the sheen of gold lettering, found stencilled above the black and white keyboard. Through the hazy spectre of the photograph could just be made out that set of characters, letters that spelled out, without a doubt, Steinway & Sons.

August 1903

Who provideth for the raven his food, when his young ones cry unto God? - Job 38:41

I f it hadn't of been for the crows, then it may have played out differently. William Wilson Kiser plodded through the corn field, sweating in the relentless heat of the North Carolina August. High above, the afternoon sun beat down like a white-hot hammer in the yellow sky. His gaze was fixed as he looked straight ahead, surrounded by the tall green corn stalks. They seemed to reach out and grab at his clothing as he paced slowly down the furrow, their arching, ribbed leaves uttering a soft, tearing whisper as their serrated edges pulled against the sweat-soaked fabric covering him. It was as though they only reluctantly let go their hold, like some garrulous old soul met on the public road, who grasps at your sleeve and leans over in order to divulge the latest news. The crows, shiny as black oil, perched themselves upon the fence rails opposite and cawed loudly their perpetual, eerily familiar jeering. He removed his battered straw hat and mopped his forehead with the bit of old sacking that he was carrying.

Beyond the field, by the side of the road, stood the low frame house, unpainted and uninviting. The pine clapboards and the cedar shingles had weathered to a sombre, uniform grey. Rough, solid shutters covered the windows in the vain attempt to shut out the summer heat, and the front porch, with coarse, splintery porch posts, stood empty and unadorned. The black square of the open front door, revealing the corner of a table covered with a fold of white tablecloth provided the sole indication of habitation. A few chickens, ruddy as the clay upon which they mechanically pecked, wandered into the dark void under the house, aimlessly re-emerging moments later. Only a ragged cedar tree out front between the house and the road, in the bare, swept yard, made any attempt to relieve the lonely aspect.

They had moved here to Providence, his wife Nancy and their four children only a few years prior, when they had returned from down east in Moore County, where he had been farming. People said the house was haunted, but he didn't know anything about such as that. What was haunted? Everything could be haunted as far as he could make out. His head was full enough already without him having to consider haints dragging chains up and down the stairs. People feared the dark of the night, but he had lain awake enough nights to know that he didn't fear any of that. It was the daytime that confounded him.

For him, the day was like the night and the

night day. He imagined it, when he could imagine, as a feed sack turned inside out, the colourful printed side facing inward and the blank white side outward. This is how it appeared, the ink, faint and backwards on the wrong side, bled through like a ghost, was all that could be made out. The dream, that tumult that he had endured so early this morning, fantastical and yet more incontrovertible than the present moment, was still haunting him, repeating itself over and over in his mind like a whirring, black machine. A dream, a nightmare, could weigh more heavily on a soul than any real occurrence could hope to do. This one clung to him like a damp, pungent sack, refusing to be shaken off.

As he wandered the corn field, crows, blue-black, black as the devil and just as cunning, watched him, hectored him. They gathered at field-edge and in the scrubby pine trees that lined the road, and like so many times before, they screeched. He paused and drank in a long look at them.

Then, like an incantation, he began to recite, "When I say my bed shall comfort me, my couch shall ease my complaint, then thou scarest me with dreams, and terrifiest me through visions."

At that, satisfied but cloyed with what had been brought to mind, with that he had just uttered, he resumed walking, the feed sack he carried swinging heavily back and forth, butting his leg.

One day, earlier in the summer, a day when the early corn was ripening, he had decided to get the shotgun and see if he couldn't shoot a few of these damned, infernal crows. He had marched up through the field and into the house, moments later returning with his Remington.

"I bet I'll get you now, you black devils," he said to himself as he pulled two shells from his trouser pocket and loaded them into the dark, awaiting chamber.

He thrust the polished wooden stock tight up to his shoulder, aimed up to the pine tree limbs out by the road, and pulled the trigger. The report echoed across the surrounding fields, the birds screaking in alarm, and the sky filled with the wild, beaten-air flapping of them taking flight. Two black bundles dropped from a limb and hit the dusty, red road like a widow's bonnet. He walked over and picked them both up by their scaly black feet. Their beaks were sharp and open and their piercing eyes black and shiny.

Carrying them out to the edge of the field, where he dropped them, he went to the barn and returned with an axe, a long wooden stob, and some twine. He drove the stob into the earth with the axe head and tied the pair of dead birds onto the top of it, hanging upside down. This was to serve as a reminder, a defiant message, to the rest of the murder of what lay in store for them. Then again, the next day, in similar fashion, he went for the gun, came out and successfully shot another. This time, he left it laying in the road, where the red dust encroached upon it and slowly dulled the black eyes and shiny jet of the feathers. Finally, days later, one of the boys, while playing, knocked it into the ditch with a stick.

On the succeeding days, he had no more success in his killing. Crows are not known for their canniness for no reason. As he would step out onto the porch, shotgun in hand, they would immediately raise the alarm and take flight. He did not stand a chance of shooting a single one. How could they know that he was about to kill them? It was as though they could read his mind. The idea of this unnerved and unsettled him greatly. Within a week he gave up altogether on his endeavour, not just annoyed but spooked at the obvious cunning of these his avowed enemies. As he worked during the day, he would brood over what he imagined to be their divinations and machinations. He would look over his shoulder as he crossed the yard, and he constantly scanned the sky overhead to detect their presence.

"From whence comest thou?" he muttered to himself, adding, "Get out from here. Get out from studying me."

However, they seemed unmoved by his exhortations.

As his mood blackened over the summer, the crows seemed to multiply and their presence became even more onerous. Then, when the early corn crop came in, not only were they a foul nuisance, but they turned destructive. They watched him, waiting until he went into the house or the barn, and when he was out of sight, they would descend on the corn field, targeting the rich, green corn stalks, stalks with their vibrant-hued leaves and their noble, plumed tassels. They tore into the neat, tightly wrapped ears of fine, yellow-brown silk, and they pillaged the tender white kernels. It was like a wild, frenzied orgy, and the sound of it was ungodly to behold. When he would return, shouting and flailing his arms and running toward the onslaught, the appointed watch crow would issue a warning, and the entire murder would flee the field, deserting the teetering, shredded stalks. Afterward, they would circle lazily overhead, drunken with the joy of plunder. They were like mocking devils to him.

Nannie appeared from inside on the front porch, her cotton apron draped over her distended belly. Placing her hand above her eyes like a visor, she scanned the expanse of farm, intent on keeping an eye on him. She was soon to give birth, and she was suffering in the August heat. Dog days are not the time to be carrying a child. She was struggling. Her younger sister Allie had lived with them when they were down east, helping with the children, especially when she was carrying Coy that few years ago, but now she herself was married, wedded to Will's youngest brother Deck. Now she had her own duties to attend to. Even so, she would have come round to help Nannie in the time up to the birth, but she had just delivered a child of her own last month. She had her hands full.

This was giving all the signs that it would not be an easy birth, and Nannie had just turned thirty-seven to boot. She was six years older than he, and with this child, she seemed to be slowing down, showing her age. She was so big in the belly as well. Another month to go and she was larger than when she had carried any of the others. The weight, the heat, and her age added together were bearing down heavily on her.

"This is not like the others Will," she said to him, her breathing laboured, as she attempted to sit herself down, "Something's different about this one. I can't put my finger on it exactly, but it don't feel the same somehow."

She had had four previously, three boys, Zeb, Braskey, and Coy and a girl, Alice Bright, so she knew what she was talking about.

Such was the concern, that his mother Eliza travelled down from Bethel Church in Cabarrus County, seat of the Kiser family, in order to look her over.

His mother came out of the bedroom, pulling stray grey hairs back into her neat bun, and declared, "That'll be twins, you mark my word. Only Providence can tell, but I believe that'll be twins."

Nearly sixty years old, she wasn't just full of idle talk either. She knew the territory. Not only had she bore six children of her own, but she had carried twins as well: Will and his brother John, they were twin boys. It could just be twins then. He knew that they, like so many things, run in families. This should have been foremost on his mind, his child or children coming. However, he couldn't keep his thoughts on it.

It all seemed to have started last spring, when

he became troubled, or more troubled than usual, roughly coinciding with planting time. However, that said, it was not a new occurrence. It had really begun, the first signs of it, down in Moore County. He had moved down there in the hopes of making something of himself, getting away from the infestation of family he had back in Cabarrus County, where the Kisers were thick on the ground. No matter where he went, there were Kisers and other of his kin: the Furrs, the Doves, the Garmons, the Howells, and the Polks. He thought that if he could just get out from under foot of them all, he could possibly breathe. He might just find out who he was.

His father was named Marcus Lafayette Kiser, but he was universally known as Fate. Fate, the Confederate veteran who suffered at the hands of the Yankees all those years ago, losing an arm in the process, was tough as old boots. He was an old man now, but even so he still lived in the shadow of his own father, Will's grandfather, John Lee Kiser, who had enlisted in the army at forty-two years of age, travelling to Raleigh to do so, in a valiant and fool-hearty attempt to prop up the dwindling and moribund Confederate forces. They, his father and grandfather, had seen so much pain, so much suffering, the deprivations and federal-sanctioned starvation after the conflict. It is not entirely surprising that they considered him, someone who could not even remember the humiliation of postbellum Yankee occupation of their homeland, much less the harrowing hellishness of the War, somehow wanting, short of the mark. Will, like all of his generation, was in their eyes, soft, lax, not enough of a man, and they didn't mind telling him as much.

They still spoke of the old man, his great-grandfather Mark Kiser, who had first seen light of day way back in the 1700's, when Cornwallis's retreating footprints were still fresh in the Mecklenburg clay. He had died within a few months of Will and his brother's birth back in 1872, which lead many, the old women, the superstitious, to speculate about the thread of connection between the passing of the patriarch and the immediate arrival of the twins. They saw it as a portent and strove to discover a mark, like a caul, on the boys to indicate a sign of the old man's imprint. Thus the boys grew up with the latent presence of the old one, one whom they had never known and had only seen, through the hazy uncomprehending eyes of an infant, for a few weeks. They had laid eyes on him, however, nevertheless.

The family savoured and remembered what old Mark Kiser had told them. He was said to have proclaimed that his own grandfather Kiser had lived and worked on the self-same banks of the Rocky River - where the family still resided - back even before the Revolution. He told how this first Kiser had been a miller, leaving the millworks to his son, Mark's father. The area was thick with family, above and below ground. They all were interred in the Kiser burial ground, some remembered with engraved stones, some with a river rock. Some were marked, others were not.

In order to escape from what he felt was his slow suffocation due to the constricting weight of family, the inescapable eye of Fate, they moved east. They had set out with Nannie's parents and two of her brothers, and in effect he had replaced his own family with hers. Down there, where the soil was sandy and the land was flat, the sun was even hotter than up here in Mecklenburg, and the ground seemed to produce less. However, the real problem was that he couldn't keep his mind on things. Whatever it was that was eating at him back home, in the midst of his own people, seemed to follow him down east, got worse even. In the end, they had to come back, not to Bethel Church, but at least closer to home. Thus, it was Providence in the end.

It was late in the spring, around planting time, that he became so distraught. Along with the distress, hand in glove with it, was the shouting. Inexplicably, he began periodically, spasmodically, when overcome by his anxiety, to scream, the noise escaping out of him like a squeal from a frightened rabbit beset by a dog. It started deep in his belly, working its way up through his gullet until he thought he would strangle on it. Only by letting it escape, wild and shrill, did he manage any relief for himself. He tried to control it, much as he could, so that it only took place out in the field, removed from the ears of his family. That way, he had only to worry about spooking the mule. But then the crows turned up, at first a pair, then an entire murder, which seemed to grow by the day. At first, when he shouted, and the mule taking it for a "gee" or a "haw" would jerk its head irritably and pull the wrong direction, the birds would fly away in fear.

With time however, their fear evaporated, and they became accustomed to his shouts, and they no longer bothered to take flight. They boldly, audaciously remained on the branches, adding their own screams to his, until he could no longer discern which squalls were his and which belonged to the clamouring birds. After some weeks of this, he slowly began to realise that their cawing was somehow metamorphosing, the very shape of it transformed into something oddly, distantly familiar. It dawned on him that their caws had come to resemble his own shouts, that as if by listening to him, they were speaking his own utterances back at him. This horrified him. He hated them and found their constant presence disturbing; they bore down on him like something heavy and hellish. In his mind, the crows were certainly mocking him.

"Get thee hence," he would direct their way through gritted teeth.

Within time, this filled his thoughts, filled his head until brimming. The internal din grew louder, more insistent each day. There was no room for anything but that which intruded immediately before him in his mind. He couldn't see around it, and he couldn't see beyond it; it was too loud, too clashing. He could only liken it to the experience of placing one of those stereopticons before your eyes, looking through the pair of ground glass lenses, and there being the photographic card there before you, the twin images of *The Assassination of President McKinley* or *The Pan American Exposition*. They floated there before you, stiff and overwhelming, but it is not those images that you strove to take in.

Therefore, you struggled to see around them, around this giant card, around the edges; that is where the world lay, off the edges. If only that card, stubbornly there before you, immovable, were not there, then you could attend to your chores, your family. You could see and you could hear. The card was not so much, to his way of thinking, a picture, like those doubled pictures of the stereopticon cards, *The Spanish American War* or *The Passing of the Indian*, but a loudness, an all-enveloping loudness so distracting that you had to fight to see around it. It was thrown up before you, tall and ponderous, sickeningly close, immoveable as stone, illegible as weathered parchment. He wondered how much louder, more cloying, it could become, or perhaps, more to the point, how much more he could endure.

His son Zeb had started to notice that things were not right. Although still a child, he was old enough to know that his daddy was acting odd. One day, when he was ploughing, he had allowed, in his distraction, the mule to wander and the row was drifting off to the left. Zeb had happened out of the barn and saw what was happening and ran up to him.

"Daddy your row's going off," he cried.

He ran up, grabbed the bit, and stopped the

wayward beast.

"What's wrong Daddy?" he asked, a troubled expression knitting the brows on his boyish face.

Will ventured to laugh it off, to make it all into a joke, but his son was not taken in an attempt as clumsy as this.

After he had come to the realisation that employment of the shotgun would no longer prove useful or successful, he had come upon another idea. With this in mind, he had travelled up to Bethel Church where his mother and father lived, indeed where all his family had lived for countless generations. He had hitched up the mule to the wagon and made his way through Indian Trail and up the Indian Trail Road to Cabarrus County. Traversing the old roads that he knew so well, he arrived at a pleasant grove where a modest but comfortable old frame house snuggled amongst the old oak trees. It could not have been less like the place he had just left back in Providence. His father Fate, carrying what looked to be a half-gallon jar of molasses in his remaining arm, was heading up to the front porch where his mother Eliza awaited.

He alighted, and after their greeting, his father asked, "What's my prodigal son doing back up in these parts?"

"I've come on a borrowing journey," he laughed.

"Oh yeah?" he said, "I shouldn't have thought you come up here just for the company."

"I was wondering," Will continued, ignoring the slight tinge of ridicule in his father's tone, "if you still had that Colt's army revolver?"

"Yeah, I've got it," his father said, "What you asking about that for?"

"Well, I've got me some crows down at the house that've got wise to my shotgun, sorry rascals," he said. "No sooner than I come out with it, they fly off."

"Well it's a fine day when your own flesh and blood is outwitted by a pack of crows," his father said laughing. "If you can't hit the mark with a shotgun, what makes you think you can hit it with something else?"

"I was thinking I could maybe hide the pistol when I'm out in the field. That way, I could pull it out, and take them by surprise and kill me a few."

"And so you want my pistol," his father said.

"Yes, sir. I tell you what, crows about to worry me to death."

"Well, just you be careful with that old gun," his mother said.

"That's right," his father said, getting in one more dig, "Them crows are liable to get after you with that Colt's revolver, they're so smart as you allow they are."

He returned home with the gun carried in a feed sack. As he approached the house, he pulled it out and examined it. The blued metal was gleaming in the sunlight, the reflections momentarily blinding him, a silvery-blue flash on the barrel. He looked about in search of any crows, his intended target, and was not disappointed, for he saw several congregated on a fence rail in the distance. He held the pistol at arm's length, cocked it, aimed in their direction, and fired. The explosion, although not as loud as the shotgun, was enough to alarm the murder. They tore off. of the fence rail in a panic, making a huge fuss in the process, rapidly flying into the air and away from the direction of the shot. However, he did not hit a single one of them.

Nancy ran out on to the porch, as fast as she was able with her swollen ankles.

"Will Kiser, what on earth are you doing?" she demanded.

He was still staring distractedly in the direction of the fence, when she came out. He turned and looked at her, a blank expression on his face.

"Crows," he said, "crows."

"Sakes alive," she said. "Where did that gun come from?"

"Fate," he said looking down at the revolver, "old man Fate Kiser."

" And that's why you journeyed all the up to your mamma and daddy's, for a pistol? What is it about you and these crows? You're like something possessed."

The folly of it all was too much for her, and she turned to go back into the house, when a thought came to her.

"Consider the birds of the air, they neither sow nor reap nor gather into barns, and yet your Father feeds them," she said with no small import.

Thinking that was him told and nothing more need be said about it, she went inside to allow him ponder it.

They had been married for ten years now. He had only been twenty-one years old at the time they wed, and she was twenty-seven. People said that he was crazy to marry a woman that much older than himself, but his twin brother John had been married to Mary Nesbit since he was only eighteen. He was afraid that people would start talking, wondering why he hadn't already taken a wife. He had never chased after the girls like so many of them did. He had never even courted. So, when he met Nannie, and she was so willing, in fact down right anxious to marry and have a family before she got any older, it just seemed like the right thing to do.

Then before long, along came their first child, Zebulon Vance Kiser, born six months after the death of the great North Carolina patriot for whom he was named. Braskey, Bright and Coy weren't far behind, and now another one. As far as a wife was concerned, she was as good as anybody else he reckoned. A man needed to start a family and have children. That was the natural order of things. There was certainly no flying in the face of that, he thought, and there was no call for overly ruminating on man's estate.

As the years passed, the age difference between them seemed to become greater rather than less. Grey hairs were beginning to appear in Nannie's thick brown curls, and her lips were losing their colour and girlish plumpness, he noticed. When he looked at her, the future showed itself, and he could see the stirrings of an old woman. He, on the other hand, had just turned thirty-one. He was slim, and his beard was still sparse, little altered from when he was married. He still possessed the carriage and looks of a young man, that is until here recently. This spell of his, with all its worrying him like it did, keeping him awake nights, had might nigh worn him out.

As the summer progressed, the crops coming on, the heat setting in, so the insomnia, like some sort of ancient tribulation, played out. It plagued him and only seemed to exacerbate his other troubles. He hadn't slept, couldn't sleep, no matter how he tried. He lay there in the bed hour after hour, Nannie breathing slowly and softly beside him, on her back because of her great size, and tried, willed himself to sleep. It was not to happen, or if it did, it was so phantom-like that he drifted in and out of it without his even being aware of it. He listened to the clock on the mantelpiece in the front room rhythmically ticking and striking hour after hour, he heard the scratching of rats up above in the loft, of dogs down below in the cool space under the house.

He scrutinised the whole process of sleep, or lack of it in his case, until he knew every part. He was so very familiar with that feeling of being pulled slowly downward under water, of darkness turning into amorphous shapes, the shapes forming into white birds, like doves, becoming animated and speaking. He lay there and observed it, even participated in it, and yet he did not sleep. He lay there and watched the dream forming, like the image thrown up on a sheet in a magic lantern show, until he admitted to himself that he was very possibly dreaming but he was definitely, certainly not sleeping. He would then open his eyes in disgust, seeing nothing in the dark room but the blinking, blue-white spider web of his eye-veins before him.

The real dreaming seemed to occur during the day. His existence became a waking, nightmarish hallucination, like those dreams where a being repeats the same action again and again and lacks the power to stop it. People before him gave the impression of changing shape and form like fabled, demonic fantasies. The land shifted and buckled, and he sometimes became lost walking from the field to the barn. It was turned inside out. There were times that he wouldn't see a neighbour or a child even if they were standing right in front of him. He didn't hear them if they spoke, but oftentimes, on other occasions, he spoke to and reacted to something that, as far as he could discern, was right there before him.

What was it just before him? Perhaps it was the image, the voices of the big white card, slipped into his vision, like viewing existence through a pair of lenses of the stereopticon. He knew that, on the face of things, these phantoms were not there, and yet, like in a dream, they were there, and they demanded an answer. The shrill pounding that distracted him came on in the form of an endless question. It always assaulted him with a barrage, a tidal surge of a question, the exact nature of which he could not articulate. It was something turned inside out, the readable print facing the dark interior where he could not decipher it. It distracted him to the point of being dangerous. He ran into the gate one day when he should have been opening it; he nearly caught his hand in the feed mill as he was pushing ears of corn into the hopper. The grasping, oily-black teeth of the wheels nipped at his fingers, and he only narrowly escaped a serious mangling.

Today had already besieged him like the trampling of a spooked, bolting horse. Last night, he lay awake, like he did every night since he could remember. He heard the usual cracking and popping of the timber frame of the house cooling off in the warm night, and he heard the awakening of the birds before daylight. He listened to the sudden whir of brass clock wheels followed by five tormenting chimes. From what he could recollect, he had eased himself out of bed, careful not to wake the restless and uncomfortable Nannie. He dressed and tiptoed out of the front door and suddenly found himself standing at the edge of the corn field, midday sun bright above him.

He turned and there in front of him, with a drape of white behind them were two men, standing side by side, the look and handsomeness of which he had never before in his life beheld. They were as identical in countenance and dress as ever he had seen. As they came closer to him, either one stepped behind the other, or maybe he slipped behind Will himself, but as to how this happened, he could not fathom. Perhaps it was only one man all along, but there hovering right in front of him was this man, almost glowing in green and gold. He was tall and well-shaped with gold whiskers and hair, and his eyes were a wonderful greyish purple, the colour of an evening, just before dark. He had placed upon his head a fine, braided, yellow straw hat, with a jaunty tassel placed in the hatband. Even Solomon in all his glory was not arrayed like one of these, he thought.

Will could not recognise him, and yet he seemed, somehow or another to know him.

"Consider the birds of the air," he was saying.

He looked down and the man was holding an ear of sweet corn, ripe and white. The man smiled and offered it to him, and he thought to reach out and take it, but found that he was unable to lift his arms.

Why can't I move? he asked.

Then he looked down, and saw that he had been bound, his body tied by baling twine to a large stob driven down into the earth of the field.

When he looked back up, the man was gone, but he sensed that someone was behind him. He thought it could be the remarkable man, but when he craned to see, he discovered his brother John, there on the stob behind him. He scanned left and right, searching for the beautiful man, and it was then that he noticed crows all about, crows in the pines, crows on the ragged, rotten fence rails, crows flying overhead, shiny as oil. Their cawing was deafening, although it seemed that they were speaking in human voices, in voices that he could recognise. He looked down again and saw that they, the crows were on him, pecking at him and tearing at his clothing. There were three, four, he didn't know how many. He struggled to free himself but could not.

Meanwhile, the crows continued in their attack, ripping through his trousers, shredding the fabric, until they reached his silky, yellow-brown hair, tearing it out in great clumps.

He screamed, desperate and shrill, "Get out from me. Get out from me."

In their frenzy, they stripped back the tender skin of his manhood with their reptilian claws. All the while he was powerless to stop them and could only watch helplessly. They savagely plucked at the tender kernels of his seed, piercing it with their ravenous beaks and gorging on the oozing, milky contents. He let out a wild shriek, while he attempted to shake them off. He was shaking uncontrollably, when he awoke violently, like a window shade snapping up, Nannie's face over him.

"Will, Will, wake up," she was shouting as she shook both his arms.

He was covered with sweat and panting. He looked like a wild man, terrified and possessed, and he stared at her as though he had never known her.

Come midday, he sat down to the table where streaked meat, peas, and cornbread were awaiting. The noise in his head was pounding, beating to the point that he did not notice his wife there in the kitchen, did not notice his children around the table, did not take in the food before him. He sat looking out of the open door, absentmindedly sipping his coffee from the saucer.

"Will, what's ailing you?" Nannie asked. "You've barely touched your dinner"

"Hmm?" he said as he looked up, "Nothing."

"You walk around here like you've seen a haint or something."

"There's no haints around here."

"Well, I can't quite figure it, but you haven't been right for a good while now," she said. "You act like you're looking at something, like there's something standing there in front of you and you can't get shut of it. I know that much."

"I don't see nothing," he said, standing up and leaving the table.

He spent the rest of the day out in the fields or in the barn, stopping only for his supper. He ate his cornbread and milk in silence, then returned to the fields, where he now walked. As the sun descended, the limbs of the trees, the fence rails, and the roof ridge of the barn, had become populated with crows, crows cawing and fighting. A verse continued to course through his head.

Then thou scarest me with dreams, and terrifiest me through visions: So that my soul chooseth strangling, and death rather than my life, he repeated.

Armed with this, he left the field, carrying the feed sack, and walked up to the front porch and climbed the steps. There he took the lone straight chair with a sagging splint seat and sat down on it.

He reached into the sack and pulled out the

revolver, dark and blue, and laid it in his lap. Zeb and Braskey were out playing in the dusty front yard. Braskey had a stick and was rolling a barrel hoop, and Zeb was hitting rocks out into the road with an old broom handle. Presently, little Coy came toddling out, followed by Bright, and then by Nancy.

The children ran over to their father, who put an arm around each of them, as Nannie called out to the other two, "Boys, come in the house now, it's time for bed before long."

She looked out across the fields and said, "I wonder what is troubling those birds so? What a commotion."

She turned toward him and said, "What are you doing with that old gun?"

"Crows, crows, goddamn crows," he said, not looking up.

"Shush up, little jugs have big ears," she chided. "Those crows will fly off to their roost in a little while, just like they do every night without any help from you. Providence will see to that."

"Providence," he said looking up at her for the first time. "Do you reckon this here Colt's army revolver is Providence if it blows seven bells out of something?"

"You can make fun if you want to Will Kiser, but there's no flying in the face of what is ordained."

"Nancy Louise, I'm not making fun, with God as my witness I'm not. I just can't figure it out," he said.

He looked back down to his lap and continued, "Why is light given to a man whose way is hid, and whom God hath hedged in. Seems like there's Providence and then there's fate."

"All I know is, the ways of man are before the eyes of the Lord, and he pondereth all his goings. You'd do well to remember that, Will Kiser," she said, her hackles up.

"Boys, I said come in now," she said raising her voice.

She then softened.

"Those crows don't take any notice of that old gun anyhow. They seem to have got you figured right out, and I wish to heavens I could say the same for myself."

At this she took the two little ones by the hand, turned, and stepped on the threshold, followed by Zeb and Braskey.

"Anyhow," she said, "all this sad talk don't do a soul any good."

He looked up at her, and said, "Do you think that a man can be marked?"

"They say in the final days, man will have a mark on the forehead. I don't understand all that. Just you remember, even the hairs on your head are numbered...Don't stay out here too long."

"No," he said, "I won't."

Dusk was setting in, and crickets, cicadas, and tree frogs were singing their evening song along with the cacophonous din of the crows. It boiled and pounded in his head until he was fairly reeling.

He looked down at the rough plank floor and

matter-of-factly said, "Stop."

The sun was going down behind the trees on the horizon and the sky shone an orange-red. Still, the crows were gathered in the scraggy pines by the road and by the barn. He was drawn into the noise, completely absorbed by it. He tried to look beyond it, around it, but he could not. His breathing became short and shallow as he attempted to peer around it, to see around the edges of it.

If he could just have seen around it, this big looming card with the twinned images on it, then he could have breathed easily. He could have attended to the things that he needed to attend to. He could have thought about Nannie and the child she was carrying, maybe the children she was carrying. It could be twins like his brother and himself. Things run in families. The cawing of the birds was familiar to him, it resembled his own desperate shouting out in the fields. The crows had listened to it and were now shouting it back at him. If only, God in heaven, they would stop. If it would stop, he could see around it, and then he could know. If only it would have stopped demanding, stopped pushing, stopped asking.

Once more, he pleaded, "Stop."

Dusk was coming on quickly now, and the sky was turning that purple-grey colour of corn smut, and the scabby pines were transformed into dark silhouettes. He picked up the pistol from his lap and stood up. Lifting the chair by its back rail, he swung it around and placed it neatly against the wall by the front door. He saw the feed sack laying on the floor and noticed that when he had removed the pistol, he had turned it right side out, revealing the colourful, printed logo. Slowly descending the weathered steps, he walked through the bald yard, past the cedar tree and out into the road. It stretched long and straight to the darkening horizon of Providence, where it vanished from sight.

He said, "The eye of him that hath seen me shall see me no more: thine eyes are upon me, and I am not."

A few of the crows lifted off of the their perches and proceeded to fly off. These few were soon joined by others, all flapping their wings and taking flight, all heading in the same direction, cawing loudly as they did so, flying to their roost, somewhere off over the horizon. Then, within a few moments, the entire murder took to the air, flying overhead like black oil spinning off of the wheels of a whirring farm machine. At this he lifted the gun, it's blueness like the onset of the evening sky. The maelstrom in his head had ceased its swirling and pounding. No more was the question beating, beating on his chest. He could no longer see around the edges, nor did he feel the need to. His vision was covered, complete. He raised the revolver, without looking at it, without seeing the road, without seeing the crows passing overhead, and turned it to his head.

The Healer

B y anyone's reckoning, it was a desperate errand. Slowly, hesitantly, a battered old Nash touring car rolled into the gravel driveway behind the house. It was a tall, square auto, of the type popular in the previous decade. As it pulled to a stop, the brakes squeaked and the motor uttered a desperate-sounding gasp as it cut out. From the back of the white, clapboard house, Gwen Kiser, fair-skinned and redheaded, glanced out of a kitchen window, opposite the sleeping porch.

"Good gracious, who could that be?" she said craning her neck over the table and wiping her petite hands on a dish towel.

Presently, a man climbed out of the car. He was wearing dusty, denim overalls and a dirty striped shirt with no collar, the lack of which accentuated his leathery, sunburned neck. On his head sat a crumpled, shapeless black hat. Then, from the other side of the vehicle, a thin, weary-faced woman placed one of her down-at-the-heel black oxfords on the running board and slowly stepped down, looking warily about her from under her old cloche hat. She was carrying a pale, tow-headed child not more than a few years old, on her hip. The man motioned with one arm for the woman to precede him up the stepping stones, through the tall oaks, toward the wooden step and high, back door of the house.

"Lands," Gwen said, watching intently, "I wonder what on earth....but I think I can tell you right now what this is going to be."

She put the dishtowel down and untied her apron just as she heard a knocking on the heavy, latticework, back porch door. She stepped out onto the latticed porch, and pushing open the door, saw the couple standing at the bottom of the steps. The man had on worn-out brogans, like country people wore.

"Excuse me ma'am," he said, "Is this where Mr. Will Kiser lives?"

"Mr. Kiser's my husband," Gwen said with a tinge of haughtiness, not pronouncing the "r" on the end of the surname, a custom she had picked up since moving to town.

She noticed that the woman's print dress was faded and threadbare. The child was exceptionally wan and did not look well.

"Name's Wallace ma'am. We're from down below Providence, down Weddington way, and folks down there has allowed that Mr. Will Kiser is the man we want to see. Our young'un here has got the thrash, ma'am, and we was hoping Mr. Kiser could kindly see to him."

"Well, I thought as much" Gwen said, looking at them a little dubiously.

There being nothing they could say in response, they simply stood there, looking at her with the slow patience that is learned from a life that has not been granted the luxury of expectation.

Then softening somewhat she added, "Well, seeing as you've come all this way, I'll go see if I can find Mr. Kiser for you."

She turned around and let the door slam behind her.

"Thank-you kindly ma'am," the man said to the latticework.

She directed herself up the hallway to the front room, calling, "Daddy, there's some people from Weddington out on the back steps with a baby that's come down with the thrash. They're wanting to see you."

Will Kiser was smoking a cigar while seated in a mohair easy chair that was placed by the large, freestanding, walnut radio. The radio console was of the type that resembled a Gothic church altar.

"Weddington?" he shouted, "Who are they?"

He had relations who lived down in Weddington.

"I don't know. Nobody you'd know from the looks of them," Gwen said, "And nobody you'd want to know either."

"You didn't bring them in the house?" Will asked.

"Good gracious no," she said, putting a hand on her hip.

"Well Mama, what's got into you?" he chided as he placed his cigar on the little mahogany smoke stand by the chair and stood up.

He strode down the hallway, out the back porch, and down the steps to the waiting couple.

"How do sir; how do ma'am," he bellowed.

He shook the man's hand vigorously and nodded to the woman.

"I'm Will Kiser. What can I do for you today?"

He was tall and had a good head of curly hair, like Rudy Vallee.

"How do sir, my name's Fate Wallace, and this here is my wife Sadie," the man began, encouraged by Will Kiser's reception.

"Mr. Kiser, we come up here today in hopes of seeing you."

He paused, as though to gather his pitch.

"I'm not going to beat around the bush, sir; I'm going to tell you like it is. This here baby of ours is bad with the thrash, Mr. Kiser. That's the reason for us turning up here on your doorstep like we did. Folks down in Weddington gave us your name. They allow as how you have the gift of curing the thrash. Mr Kiser, they say you are a healer."

"Well a good many believe that," Will said, scratching the back of his head, "but I don't know if I'd put too much stock in all that. I declare I don't."

"But is it like they tell, Mr Kiser, that you never seen your own daddy?" the man said.

"Yes that is right," Will conceded, knowing where this was going and reluctantly resigning himself to it.

"I never did see my own daddy. He died a month before I was born."

"I'm sorry to hear that sir, but if what you say is so, then that means you have the gift. You have the power to cure this here child of ours," the man said.

"If he's bad off, then you ought to get a doctor to see him," Will said, running a hand through his hair.

The man looked at his wife, then down at the ground.

"A doctor's not something we got the money for," he said. "People say you got the gift Mr. Kiser. If you would just put the cure on him, then folks say he'd heal. He'll be right as rain. Them who knows, say it's so."

"Like I said, I wouldn't go putting much stock..," Will said but stopped himself when he studied the face of the man, and then that of the woman, at the longing desperation so evident in both.

They kept looking intently, pleadingly at him. He well knew, that for them, for poor country people like these with no chance of seeing a doctor, that this was the closest that they could hope for, for a cure for their child.

"Well, I don't suppose it would hurt," he finally conceded, "but I don't want to go putting any false hopes in your head."

"Any hope's better than no hope Mr. Kiser," the man said, 'but I tell you this, we do believe."

"All right, but we should pray over him too don't you think? After all, it is only the Lord who can heal."

"Yes sir, we know that it's the Lord what give you the gift of healing, Mr Kiser. We don't deny that for one minute." the man said.

"Come here sonny boy," Will said, stretching out his arms and taking the child from the mother.

His arm acting as a seat, he tucked the child, facing him, comfortably against his own ribs.

"Let's see here," he said.

He took his left thumb and gently pulled down the child's chin, opening the mouth. He then craned his neck down and blew slowly and steadily into the child's mouth for nearly half a minute. He removed his thumb, the mouth still gaping for some moments afterward. The child stared at him with a grave expression on his face. Had he not been so sickly and weak, he no doubt would have protested or cried. However, as it was, he could only muster a perplexed glare.

"Let's bow our heads," Will said, the couple dutifully obeying.

"Heavenly Father, we ask you to bless this child, that he may be touched by your healing hand, and we ask you Father to restore him to health and to be anointed in your divine grace and in your infinite love. We ask this Father, through Jesus Christ our Saviour, Amen."

"Amen," repeated the woman. "Thank-you sir. That was an awful perty prayer."

"Thank-you Mr. Kiser. We're much obliged," added her husband, as he took the child and handed it back to its mother. "As for paying you..."

"Now I don't want any money, not a dime,"

Will said fiercely, "If you really think it's a gift, then I don't have any business charging for it. You just work on getting this child better. You hear me?"

"God bless you Mr. Kiser," the woman said.

Then looking upward and wiping a tear from her eye, she added, "and God bless you ma'am."

Unbeknownst to Will Kiser, his wife had stepped outside and was standing at the top of the steps.

"I hope your little boy gets well soon," Gwen said.

The woman smiled and turned back toward the car, followed by her husband. When they reached the end of the path, they both looked back, silently, for a moment.

"Y'all take care now," Will said, watching them retreat into the shabby old Nash.

As the old automobile struggled to a grinding start, Will Kiser turned to his wife and said, " We don't even begin to know how some people live. Do we Mama?"

"We sure don't, Daddy; we sure don't," Gwen said.

After the car had turned onto the main road and disappeared, she added, "And I declare, after you touching that child, if we don't all come down with the itch, then I don't know what."

She quickly turned and stomped off, letting the door slam behind her, leaving Will Kiser at the bottom of the steps, smiling to himself, saying, "Oh Mama."

The Photograph

S ome things are not readily explained. For instance, what is in a picture? What precisely is a photograph? Is it simply a moment, a bit of light captured, via chemical means, onto a scrap of paper? And through the medium, before it darkens, fades, and crumbles, we are allowed a glimpse of that moment? Just as the pinhole of the camera permitted the light to seep in and create the negative, so we are allowed a pinprick's view into the past. It is fleeting, transient, and malleable: the image is altered, and our understanding is uprooted and it tumbles headlong. We may be enlightened, or more than likely, we are cast into darkness. Even so, we beaver on, heads down, constructing our past. How many words is a picture really worth?

When I was growing up in North Carolina, I spent a good deal of time with my grandmother. She had for years been used to having people around her, my grandfather and her own aged mother, my great-grandmother. Then, in 1970, my grandfather died rather suddenly and unexpectedly. A few months later, my great-grandmother died at the incredible age of one hundred and two. Thus, in less than a year, my grandmother found herself all alone, more than a little frightened, and with little to do. Perhaps it was my parents who struck upon the idea that I go and stay the nights with her; I don't remember, but so began that period of my childhood when I was very frequently at her house and in her company.

I was an odd and somewhat timid little boy, who given the choice, preferred the company of an old woman to that of children my own age. Being with my grandmother suited me fine, and slowly, my presence and companionship began to fill the ragged gap in her life left by the sudden departure of her husband and mother. We watched television together, took meals, played cards, and played the piano together. We always slept in the same bed, and I remember - this seems almost incredible now - the gun that lay under my pillow every night. She kept it beside her when she slept, ostensibly as a means of protection, and so when I was there, it was under *my* pillow. I was too frightened even to look at it, but I knew that it was there all the same, under my head, under my pillow.

She said to me, "Now Sonny, don't mess with that pistol. We're liable to get shot."

To this day, I don't know if it was loaded or not, but my inclination is to think that it was. I didn't consider it anything out of the ordinary. I figured that everyone's grandmother kept a gun in the bed.

There was at her house, in the back bedroom,

under the bed, a large, flat, metal box. Periodically, on an afternoon, she would take me back to this room and we would pull the box out, lift the latches, and raise the metal lid, resting it against the side of the bed. Inside, the box was filled, packed with old photographs. Pulling them out of the box one at a time, she would begin the process of telling me who each person portrayed was. There were photographs of my father, my uncle, my aunt. There were photographs of my grandmother and grandfather years before, in the 1920's. There were pictures of cousins, great-aunts and uncles, and there were pictures of my sainted great-grandmother from the 1880's onwards. I learned to recognise the likeness of my great-grandfather, the "Jack of all trades" and my great-great grandfather, the Civil War Veteran.

The picture that made the greatest impression on me was a rather large photograph, about eight by ten inches, mounted, in typical fashion for the time, on a larger piece of card stock, which surrounded the image like a mat. This picture, I remember, was not in a particularly good condition, the card having been bent and broken off at the corners, lending it a ragged, crumbly appearance. The creases had encroached into the photograph itself, and had eroded and destroyed bits of the image. The subject was of an old house, an unpainted, single-storey, farm house with empty porch running along the front. The roof was covered in rough wooden shingles. Sitting in front of this house on a collection of straight chairs with splint seats was a family group. There were five children, ranging in age from around six to about fourteen years. The two youngest of the lot were obviously twin boys, dressed in identical velvet suits with knee-length trousers, billed caps, and laced, ankle-height boots. They were standing on either side of a severe-faced, frowning woman who wore a high-necked blouse with puffed sleeves and a full-length, black taffeta skirt.

Pointing to one of the twins, my grandmother would say, "Now that's Daddy."

By this, she meant her husband, my grandfather. My grandparents had always referred to each other as "Mama" and "Daddy," just as in similar fashion, my father and his brother never, even until her death at the age of sixty-three, called my aunt anything but, "Sister."

"Daddy always used to tell that that old house was haunted," my grandmother would add, indicating to the dismal structure.

Indeed, I could just remember the tales my grandfather would tell, when I was just a child, the reports of the sound of chains being dragged up the stairs to the loft, of the incident when not even a breeze stirring in the dead of night, the china cabinet toppled over and came crashing onto the floor.

I would study the composition, the shadowy-looking house, the bare yard, the children, the grave mother.

"Where's his father?" I would ask.

"He died," she would say, "before Daddy was born. He never even *saw* his own papa."

With this, she would take the picture from me and place it in the pile, turning her attention to the next one awaiting.

It was only years later, that I learned the exact circumstances of my great-grandfather's death. It was a shock to hear that he had committed suicide, turning a pistol to his own head, not even a month before my great-grandmother gave birth to twin boys on the tenth of September 1903. There was a short article about it in a local newspaper, the cool objectivity of which, to this day makes the hair stand up on the back of my neck. It reads in part, "The deed was done in the public Road almost in the presence of the man's family, and no explanation of it or a probable motive has been suggested, except a mere belief that his mind was unbalanced..."

One can imagine, that once I was in possession of this knowledge, I never regarded that photograph in the same way again. I would study the house, to see if I could identify it, from its very appearance, as the sad home of a family having been confronted with a suicide, as a place of straightened circumstances, the lot of those who have no head of house to farm, to bring in an income. The idea of it being haunted took on a broader dimension and a more profound possibility. I scrutinised the faces of the children, to see if I could uncover any tell-tale signs which indicated their trauma or sadness. I would peer deeply at my great-grandmother's face, into her eyes, trying to discern, to detect any sign of her loss, of what must have been her unfathomable pain. Was there something tangible that I could sense?

I wondered, as she sat there unflinching, if she were reflecting on how he, my great-grandfather, should have been present, sitting there beside her, like in a proper family photograph. I speculated if at that very moment, when the itinerant photographer was snapping the shutter, if she was thinking about him, occupied with what he had carried out. I conjectured if this family's misfortune could in some way have been translated to the photograph itself. Had it been possible for the light of sadness to filter through the pinhole of the camera and insinuate itself onto the very fabric of the paper image? If such had been the case, did I even possess the wherewithal to recognise it, the lasting impact of a gun to the head?

As an adult, I would visit my grandmother on my returns to town and would ask if I could go back to the back bedroom and retrieve that familiar metal box. She, as is the custom in her family, lived until that venerable age of one hundred. We would perform the well-rehearsed ritual of the pictures, although in later years, I would occasionally find it necessary to prompt her as to who this or that one was, but only occasionally. One day, as we sifted through the familiar images, I came across one that I did not recognise. It was about five inches square, of a family group it appeared. I picked it up and studied it for a moment before it hit me just what it was that I held in front of me. It was the familiar image of my great-grandmother, the children, the twins on either side, but it was not the old photograph that I had beheld so intently in the past. It had been reduced in size, cut down. There was no longer any view of the lonely, sad old house with the rough shingled roof.

To all accounts, as far as I could see, my grandmother had been at work. Apparently, at some time since I had last viewed it, she had decided to tidy this old photograph up, to get rid of the broken corners and bent card by means of a pair of scissors, and in the process she had discarded the majority the photograph itself.

"What on earth have you done?" I shouted.

"Well Sonny," she said, "that old thing was such a mess."

"Well it's not like it was out here with somebody looking at it every day," I said, trying to conceal my rapidly growing anger.

Of course, by this time, it was too late, the act, the editing had already been done. As exasperated as I was, I knew it was pointless to argue with one's ancient grandmother.

I have that picture now, in its diminished state. I have all the old pictures, the only things of importance from my grandmother's estate that were portable enough for me to put into a trans-Atlantic suitcase. I still pull it out and examine it, look into my great-grandmother's face, and with my age, my lengthening expanse of experience, I attempt to uncover some slight clue in her stern expression, evidence of the act my great-grand-father had carried out so many years ago, but which at that time was still fresh and raw. On top of that, I try to recall the breadth of incommodious house, the empty porch, the image that used to exist beyond the bounds of the present, neatly-cropped, intentionally excised edges. I become irritated at not being able to remember it. The photograph piques me, as well as rankles me. It is an object perplexing in that it holds two mysteries. One mystery is the obvious one, of the reasons my great-grandfather was so distraught, in so much anguish, that he found suicide, a month before the birth of his sons, his only discernible course of action.

There is another mystery as well, for as the years had come and gone, it had become evident that I was going the be the recipient of the old family photographs. Therefore, I can't help but to contemplate my grandmother, and what she was thinking, what would have been weighing so strongly on her mind, that she would push her frail frame up from the chair, hobble to her ancient Singer, open the drawer, and pull out her rusty old shears. What would be so pressingly insistent that she would go to an unused part of her house, a room that she didn't even bother to heat, and somehow manage to extract this large and bulky box out from under the bed? What would be so imperative on her that she needed to pore through the stacks of old photographs, photographs untouched for years (and then only by she herself) and choose the one that she had been ruminating about, the one that had been troubling her so? What was going through her head when she pulled it out and cut, with difficulty, a neat square into the dusty card with her arthritic old hands, and disposed of the creased, messy, untidy parts? This is the mystery.

It had been a century nearly, since that photo had been taken. There was no one alive any longer who had ever even laid eyes on that sad, ramshackle old house. Why then, after so many years, did my grandmother feel the need to intervene, to edit, to literally cut out and dispose of a part of one of the last visual reminders of a past, a past that was slowly, without any help from her, decaying and turning to dust? How was it that the need to go in, to clean up a battered, frayed past, was so strong that she, so late in the day, felt she had to intrude? My grandmother is no longer with us, and whatever motives she had, acting as she did, she took to the grave with her. No matter how long I scrutinise it, I know that I will never, as long I live, hold the answer to this. I can stare at the photograph from now until doomsday, and I intend to do just that, but I will never know. There are some things that a picture simply cannot tell you.

The Antique Dealer

T oday was going to be the appointed day. I peered out of the soot-covered window at the gaudy market across the street below, where a small Korean man was dousing the sidewalk out front with buckets of water. I had made my mind up. Today was going to be the day that I walked over to that antique shop in the Village, went in, and introduced myself to the owner. I had determined that this was what I was going to do even before I had moved to New York, and now I had been here three weeks to the day. I had been thinking about it all this time and had decided, had gotten my courage up, to do it. I would go in, casually introduce myself and tell the owner, this Mr. Bowen, that we had a friend in common.

I chose my clothes with care, not wanting to come across as a rube, which would have been all too easy to do, as I was, for all my pretensions, still an obvious provincial. I had given away tons of clothing before I left North Carolina, thinking it inappropriate for the City, and had bought new, assuming that it would be just the thing, only to realise within a few weeks that what I had gotten rid of would have passed, and what I had just bought was hopelessly wrong. I had a lot to learn. Furthermore, I wanted to come across as though I had simply popped in, was just passing by this shop, and what I was wearing was of no consequence, no more planned, no more studied than was, to all appearances, the visit. It takes so much thought to look as though you put no thought into something. I methodically ironed a shirt.

Leaving the tiny, crumby apartment with the bath in the kitchen that I was subletting over in the East Village, I was bound westward. The area was not so gentrified then. Late at night, from my dirty window overlooking Avenue A, I could routinely see winos sleeping rough out on the street. Those were the days of the East Village "bar" bars: Crow Bar, Boy Bar, Tunnel Bar, Wonder Bar. Closely observing the men in the bars and on the street, I had already been to St. Mark's Place and had my hair shaved and cropped like a proper East Village male.

"Very nice," the young Russian barber said, congratulating me on my new, urban look. I was in the centre of it all.

It was October, and I remember that the weather was gorgeous, cool nights and warm days with brilliant, ridiculously blue skies, a welcome change from the incessant, debilitating heat of North Carolina. The leaves were colouring beautifully. A few days earlier, I had walked across the Brooklyn Bridge, and not knowing what to do once I had arrived in Brooklyn Heights, had immediately turned around to walk back to

Manhattan. The sun was setting behind the great stone piers of the bridge, the Twin Towers, and the other the downtown buildings by that hour, and it was all glorious beyond words, a moment to remember. I arrived back to Avenue A glowing with contentment. Today however, I had something else that I needed to do.

Each block gradually became nicer than the preceding one as I progressed toward the more salubrious Greenwich Village where the shop was located. I knew where it was, as I had already scouted it out in the confusing jumble of streets that make up the area, where West 4th Street is known to somehow cross West 4th Street at one point. I had searched for it within a day or two of arriving in the City, in anticipation for my eventual visit there. After crossing the wide, incongruous swirling blast of Seventh Avenue, I soon approached the more sedate vicinity of the shop. It looked improbably small from the outside, located on the ground floor of a nineteenth-century building, the modest shopfront tinted green with simple, gold-painted lettering along the frieze, stating in the most understated way, "Nigel Bowen Antiques." A handwritten note on the door read, "Please ring for entry." This was not a practice we had down South, not something I had encountered before, and I found it a bit intimidating, but taking a deep breath, I pushed the button and was greeted with a buzzing which I guessed to be my cue to push the door handle.

Once I entered, it took a few seconds for my

eyes to adjust from the outside brilliance to the low lighting inside. In the interim, I noticed the sound of a voice, a man's voice, and was initially disconcerted as to whether it was directed to me or to someone else. In the confusion, I shouted, "Hi," only to realise when I had no response that it was not for me at all. I could feel my cheeks burning in embarrassment, and I hoped whoever it was had not heard me. Only as my eyes became accustomed to the room, could I see from where this voice came, on the far side of the space, in the corner. Behind an antique desk sat an older man, greying hair and ruddy face, talking on the telephone, an old, black rotary-dial phone. He spoke with an accent, but I couldn't make out what sort. Growing up in North Carolina does not give you any advantages when it comes to recognising accents, and Jax didn't ever mention that this Nigel was foreign. He didn't acknowledge me in any way, that is other than having just buzzed me into the shop, which left me feeling a bit awkward. I was only beginning to understand the habits of New York.

While he continued - he and whoever was on the other end were talking about someone and a weekend and an upcoming dinner or something - I looked around the shop and was immediately overwhelmed by its contents, the simple exterior giving no hint as to the dazzling sumptuousness that bombarded you once inside. It was full, very full, and yet orderly. Within a few moments I could see that it was not just any old common-variety antique shop, such as I was used to back home, but one that specialised in the high-end and the neoclassical. All about me were arranged English sabre-leg chairs, Continental Biedermeier fall-front secrétaires, and marble-topped Empire centre tables. On every surface there sat urns and busts in Greek and Roman style, and on nearly every inch of the walls were hung engravings of entablature and temples, all framed in black and gold. There were leather boxes stacked in pyramids, neatly folded Paisley shawls in red and orange, and tea caddies in the shape of sarcophagi. It was rich with the lustre of mahogany and the sheen of ormolu.

This Mr. Bowen, if this was indeed he, made no haste to end his telephone conversation, leaving me to browse around the shop, which made me more than a little self-conscious.

"Oh no, she's impossible that one is," he was saying, "legless she was."

I never know what to do in such situations. You do your best to look interested in the goods before you, but not knowing how long the person with whom you wish to speak will be, you are not sure of the amount of time to pause and scrutinise anything. There is nothing worse than going round the entirety and then still being faced with a wait. My palms were getting sweaty. I tried not to reveal that I was listening to his conversation, or not so much his conversation but his speech, to determine where he was from. At first I thought it was English, only to decide within a few moments that it was not quite that. I finally concluded that it must be Irish, although how I arrived at this I have no idea.

Eventually he said his good-byes, placing the receiver on the hook.

Then looking up at me, at once grave, he said, "Yes."

It was not unfriendly, but it was not exactly inviting either.

I walked over to the desk, and a little too spritely, a little too energetically, I said, "Hello. Are you Mr. Bowen?"

"That I am," he answered, unmoved by my attempts at friendliness.

He had that look on his face that people get when they know they are about to be hit up for money.

"Hi," I continued with forced enthusiasm, "My name is Will Kiser."

His expression remained fixed, which made me feel that I had better state my business sooner rather than later.

"I've recently moved here from Greensboro, North Carolina," I said, "and I believe we have an acquaintance in common. I mean, we have a friend in common, um, we had a friend in common."

He said nothing, but did raise one eyebrow to communicate he had at least heard me. He certainly wasn't making this any easier. Perhaps this had all been a mistake.

"Yes sir," I rattled on, like someone selling magazines door to door, "I believe we had a friend in common. I think you knew Jax Brogdan? I think he used to work for you? That's what he said, that he used to help out here in the shop."

His face began to change, soften somewhat, and he relaxed his position in his chair a bit.

"He moved down to Greensboro you know, and that's where we met," I said.

After what seemed like an interminable pause, he at last spoke.

"So he did," he said. "And he was a friend of yours, was he?"

"Yes sir, he was a neighbour of mine," I rattled on.

"And where was it you said?"

"Greensboro," I said, and when he didn't show any sign of recognition, I added, "North Carolina."

Christ, it's not that remote, I thought.

"Oh yes, I remember it was somewhere down there, South Carolina. His sister is there I believe?"

"North Carolina, yes, yes his sister, she lives there, uh down there," I said.

"What did you say your name was again?" he asked, the gruffness melting away from his voice.

"Will Kiser," I said smiling.

"And you seem to know I'm Nigel Bowen," he said with mock surprise as he lifted himself slightly out of the seat and offered me his hand.

I uttered an internal sigh of relief.

Jesus, finally, I told myself.

"Yes sir, Jax spoke of you a lot," I said. "And we worked together as well, for a while, before..."

At this I hesitated slightly.

"Before he died?" he said in what I thought to be a disarmingly matter-of-fact manner.

"Uh, yes, before he...died," I fumbled.

I wasn't sure, but I felt as though I were blushing.

At last, he formed what could be interpreted as some sort of smile, motioned with his hand, and said, "Have a seat."

College Hill was the colourful, if somewhat down-at-the-heel, Greensboro neighbourhood adjacent to the university, where I was a graduate student. The tree-lined streets were crowded with old and decaying but charming Victorian and Edwardian houses, which had been broken up into apartments offering cheap rent. If the city had a bohemian quarter, then this was it. It was here that I first spotted Jax Brogdan. He had moved in two doors down from the run-down apartment house on Tate Street where I rented a rambling, peeling apartment. I had noticed him because he was new to the area - the neighbourhood was small - and no doubt because of his looks. He was handsome and obviously, from what I could discern by his haircut and clothing, not a local. It was only later, at the shop where I had a part-time job while I leisurely worked on my master's thesis, that I first met him. He had come in to buy some flowers, and my employers had struck up a conversation with him.

Of course they had already heard about him. Greensboro was not a large city, and the gay grapevine had short but thoroughly encompassing branches. Word had gotten round that a sexy new man had moved to town, from New York no less.

Thus, by the time he ambled into the shop that afternoon, he had already cut a figure, had turned the heads of numerous local gay men. This was I suppose, I was to learn later, his chief talent. I, on the other hand, could have walked down South Elm Street buck-naked at high noon and no one would have even looked up. That day I met him, he was quiet, polite, and wearing an exotic-looking necklace of multi-coloured beads.

When I asked about his unusual name, he said, "It's short for Jackson, but I spell it with an X."

Of course he would, I would later come to think. He shook my hand and left with his paper-wrapped bundle of flowers.

After that day, I diligently attempted to run into him whenever possible. Our apartments both backed onto an unpaved service alley, which was directly overlooked by his back door. Therefore, wherever I went, I somehow managed to pass by, even going out of my way to do so. "Oh, I'm just going to the gym," I would gush if I happened to catch him outside watering his plants or taking out his rubbish. After a few weeks of these not so spontaneous meetings, he invited me in to his apartment one day, and I saw that he was living with a bed, a chair, a television, and not much else. Probably at what I saw as an opportunity to insinuate myself into his life in some way, I offered to help him make his surroundings a bit more comfortable, although he never mentioned or suggested that his living situation was lacking in any way.

However, that did not stop me, and I took on the filling up of Jax's apartment as a sort of project. And by extension, I can see now, I suppose I took on the filling up of Jax's life with myself as a project as well. So I, the packrat who kept myself busy in all the antique and junk shops downtown, proceeded to provide him with cutlery, crockery, lamps, electric fans, whatever he did not have. As he possessed practically nothing, it was easy to supply him with household goods. I even lent him a chair so that I could have a place to sit when I visited. Along with the goods, came my rather insistent company and companionship. Thus, by degrees, we became friends of sorts.

Gradually, I learned his story, of how he had lived in New York, had a wealthy boyfriend, ran with a fast crowd, took copious quantities of drugs, knew the rich and the famous. He spoke of weekends in the Hamptons and hanging out with Debbie Harry, and I drank it all in. Who could blame me? I who lived nowhere, I the skinny, I the not handsome, and I the poor. I did happen to notice that what he never seemed to mention in his New York stories was work or a job. Looks are a very powerful means to get you what you want, and from reading between the lines, I gathered that Jax had been very adept at using them and getting what he wanted. It seems that he had lived well.

Of course that was all in the past (how long ago I never learned), and now he sat in a half-empty apartment in the unrelenting Greensboro heat. How he had fallen from the high life, of which he spoke so frequently, to the decidedly meagre existence that I saw before me, he never divulged, and I, being brought up with rural manners, thought it better not to ask. The only clue he offered about it all was the state of his health. Although you certainly would not know it to look at him, he was, by his own admission, not well.

All he said to me was, "You know I'm positive."

"Oh, really," I answered, feigning nonchalance.

I wanted him to think that this was no big deal, something I heard every day, but in reality I was quite shocked by what he had revealed. He was the first person I knew (while I knew them) who was HIV positive. Although by the time I speak of, it was not the bombshell that it would have been ten years earlier, telling someone that you were HIV positive - did we still call it AIDS then? - was still a bold thing to do in a part of the country where the epidemic was more recently arrived and the fear surrounding it more pronounced. This was not New York or San Francisco. That was the only hint of an explanation he ever provided as to why he was here. Ostensibly, his health deteriorating, and without money, he moved down to North Carolina to be near his sister, who lived in Greensboro. However, as time went on, I gathered that perhaps he had been moved rather than so much willingly moving south.

Of course it did not go unnoticed by Jax that I worked for the Parson's Nose, the city's trendy antique and flower shop.

"I've been thinking about getting a job," he announced one day.

As his health was not bad enough to prevent him from going out to work a bit, and as how I worked at that "cute shop," where we had met, he wondered if I could not perhaps approach Price and Ben, the owners, about some part-time work.

By way of presenting his credentials, he said, "My ex-boyfriend wrote the definitive book on Biedermeier furniture, and I used to work for a really exclusive antique dealer in Greenwich Village."

Somehow, I doubted this was necessary for helping out at a modest little shop downtown, but obviously, I was only too glad to be considered useful enough to be imposed upon. I immediately went to my employers and asked them about hiring Jax part-time.

The Parson's Nose was one of those remarkable types of businesses that you often can find in out of the way places. Frequented by gay men, designers, and wealthy women (we called them white women, which referred to their mentality more so than their colour) it was owned by a local gay couple and was a wonderfully sophisticated, while at the same time utterly unpretentious emporium, located in the charming if crumbling antiques district downtown. Initially selling quirky antiques - all procured with Ben's incredible eye - fresh flowers were later added to the offerings in order to bring in a wider and more regular clientele. By the time of which I speak, the business was quite busy and successful, having also made a name for itself selling props for the nearby High Point furniture showrooms, and creating well-designed floristry for society parties, dinners, and weddings.

The owners could not have been more different from each other. Price, who ran the 'front of house" was loud, garrulous, an old amateur thespian with all the associated hammy qualities. He talked nonstop to everyone it seemed, connecting every random subject with the phrase, "One thing leading to another..."

Ben, on the other hand, who bought the antiques and created most of the flower arrangements back of house, was quiet, brooding, and a bit of a misanthrope. My abiding memory of him is one day, while cleaning the shop work room, he broke an old mirror. He swore, starring at the broken shards, peevishly exhaled half a cigarette's worth of smoke, and said, "Oh well, another seven years bad luck." That was Ben. The one quality this pair did share however, besides their absolute addiction to Marlboros, was their incredible kind-heartedness. Just as they had hired me a few years earlier, a penniless graduate student in need of employment, so they agreed, without hesitation, to take on Jax.

Now we not only lived adjacent to each other but also worked at the same place, and Jax and I spent more and more time together. On days that we both worked at The Parson's Nose, we rode together, either in his old car or mine. I, as you might have guessed, was completely smitten. I never spoke a word of it to him, but I'm sure it was obvious. I am notoriously bad at hiding anything, and he was no doubt incredibly well-versed in picking up the scent of infatuation buzzing about him. He, whether he knew my feelings or not, did not acknowledge them, and certainly never reciprocated in any way, never a lingering look, never a hand on the shoulder, never a word that could be interpreted as anything more than what it was.

In fact, he seemed to go out of his way to make it perfectly clear that I would never be, could never be, anything more than just an casual, slightly laughable friend.

"Myrtle," he would say, his name for me which I detested, "you are such a silly queen."

Of course he was jesting, but it cut me to the quick. Rejection I was used to - I knew I was not much of a catch, and he was really in no position to take on a new interest - but to make it so obvious that even the idea of such was preposterous, that I was something hopelessly foolish, truly stung. I didn't blame him, but that did not make it hurt any less. Still, we had a good time I suppose, for a while.

Then, it all started to come apart. Ben took me aside one day at the shop with something obviously on his mind. He nervously smoked his Marlboro.

"I don't know what to do," he said, "I know Jax is your friend, and I know he's not well and has, well you know, but when he's here, he doesn't do anything. I mean he's pretty much useless, but what do I do, Will? What do I do?"

I knew, without a doubt, that he was telling the truth. I had noticed it as well, but I guess I had chosen to ignore it in my adoration. On top of this, Jax had started to complain to me about the job, about how it was really beneath him, how he was too good to be doing the menial sort of tasks he was doing there, waiting on customers, cleaning up after the flowers. As anyone who has ever been involved in floristry knows, it is primarily about cleaning up the mess. Again, I had been sympathetic to him, choosing not to remind myself that the work he was apparently too good to do was the self-same work that I was doing most of the time.

This was not all. One afternoon not long afterward, we were standing in his living room by the window, when he motioned me over. As the sunlight streamed in, he turned his head to one side and laid a finger on his neck, where I saw a smallish, amoeba-shaped blotch.

I had an idea of what it was, but when Jax said, "It's Kaposi," it hit home.

Not knowing what to say, I said nothing. I had heard of Kaposi sarcoma, but of course I had never actually seen it. It looked harmless enough; I had seen angrier looking mosquito bites. I gathered all my courage and touched the spot, gently placing my finger upon his neck. It was the first time I had ever touched him, and I later burned with shame at the recognition that the racing of my heart was down to my touching him, and not the fact of my coming face to face, my making physical contact with the disease that was slowly killing him.

At some point, he had made the decision, when the time came, not to go on AZT, which was all that was available in those days to slow the virus. It was primitive to say the least.

"I've seen too many of my friends killed by AZT," I remember him saying, "I'm not doing that."

Of course the alternative differed little, and I wondered how many of his friends he had seen die without benefit of AZT. Before long, the one Kaposi was joined by another, and so on. As he no doubt had seen countless times before, the HIV, with nothing to stop it, was taking over. He had no control over it, which was the complete opposite of his personal relationships where he, I knew all too well, held all the cards.

Things went from bad to worse at the shop. Ben was even quieter than usual, maintaining a fixed expression on his face. Even Price seemed less gregarious. Jax did even less when he was there, if that were possible, dodging customers wanting flowers, disappearing when needed. He went from sullen to angry whenever he was asked to do anything.

To Ben's request that he do some cleaning, he testily responded, "I'm not here to sweep."

Still, neither Ben nor Price said anything. What could they say? What would they say to someone who was, in all likelihood, going to die soon. Even so, it was starting to wear thin with them, and with me. When he would leave the room, Ben and I would exchange long, knowing looks, saying nothing.

Late one afternoon, a woman came into the shop for flowers, and Jax made himself scarce, as had become usual. As I was already waiting on someone, this woman, who by the smartness of her dress looked to be on her way home from work, had to wait until I was finished before I could help her.

"I'll be right with you," I said more than once.

I was getting truly irritated, fuming and wondering just where Jax had gotten to. It was only after she had left, some minutes later that he reappeared. Apparently he had not been so far away that he did not overhear the transaction, which he found some fault with.

He laid into me, saying, "You treated that woman like she didn't have any money. It was ridiculous."

"What?" I said. "What are you talking about?"

I was confused, but primarily I was incensed. Not only was I having to wait on all the customers but was being criticised for how I was doing it.

I said to him, "So why didn't you help her then?"

"I'm not helping that woman," he said.

More words were exchanged, which became heated, and we got into a blazing argument. I'd like to say that it was evenly matched, but I gave more than I got, much more. I shouted with rage. All the simmering resentment, which had been building for weeks and months poured out. I shouted at him

133

for the tension that was omnipresent, for his indolence, for his considering himself better than us, for the awkward position he was putting Price and Ben in, and yes for his none too subtle demonstration that I would never ever be in the running as anything more than a serviceable neighbour. Of course I shouted at him for all that, but also I shouted at him for something more. I shouted at him for the festering, consuming bitterness that I harboured because he was dying. He was dying and thus was above reproach.

At the end of the day he came up to me, stoney-faced, and asked, "Are you riding home with me?"

"No I am not," I said.

We never spoke again. He quit his job at The Parson's Wife, much to the silent relief of Price and Ben, and retreated to his apartment. The virus continued its work. With nothing to slow it down, his health deteriorated rapidly. Rather than go out of my way to pass his back door, like I had once done, I went out of my way to avoid it, choosing to walk the long way around the block rather than risk running into him. Before too long, I didn't need to worry, as he was no longer at the apartment, the flowers outside withering and dying from lack of watering. He was in hospital. Then one day I heard that he had died. Several weeks later I arrived home to find all the bits and pieces that I had lent him stacked neatly on my back porch. His sister had cleared everything out. It seemed so much more stuff than I had remembered as I carried it, heavy, inside.

Several months passed, and I finally, with no more means to prevent it, gained my degree at the university, and as had been my rather unfocussed and casual plan all along, I began to do what was necessary to move to New York. I gathered up all the old and collectable possessions I had acquired in my twelve years in Greensboro: chairs, sofas, lamps, telephones, etc., and arranged for them all to be sold. I invited several antique dealers, all with whom I was friendly - everyone knew everyone downtown - to come around and buy what they would. I needed cash and I did not need all the stuff I had collected over the years.

"Come on guys," I joked with them all, "take all this shit home with you, every last bit of it."

In the end, I did pretty well from it, making some much-needed cash, but I wonder now that if a good bit of what was purchased by them they only bought simply to help me out. I can't imagine there would have been that much profit in my old goods. Strangely, it felt good to be rid of so much. I had no idea how getting rid of your possessions, things picked up over the years and held on to for some reason or for no reason at all, could feel so liberating. Within a week I said my good-byes, packed my bags, boarded the plane, and left Greensboro forever.

I took a seat by the leather-topped desk in a graceful Regency armchair, just the sort of chair that I had always wished to own myself.

"You have a very nice place here," I said.

I wanted to say something to show him, this Nigel Bowen, that I wasn't just some hillbilly up from the country, that I knew a thing or two about antiques.

"I love the pier table there. That's French?"

"Yes, bought that out of an estate near Galway. Good mirror on that one. So you know something about antiques?"

"Well, I've collected over the years, and I worked in an antique shop, in Greensboro. Nice place, but nothing as nice as this. Jax told me about your shop here, and about you, like I said. That's how I knew where to come to," I said.

Now that I had gotten through to this man, I could now focus on the reason for my visit. I felt it only appropriate to speak to him about Jax, to pay my respects in a sense. I suppose, in my eyes this was going to act as his wake of sorts. Maybe this is why I placed such importance in how and when I carried it out. Perhaps this is why I cultivated within me a certain piousness surrounding it all, obligatory and heavy. Yes, maybe this was going to be his funeral for me, and as at any funeral, I thought I would speak with the gravity and solemnity that one would expect when talking of the dead. People who have never been around death think that funerals and such are about the deceased, but I think they are not. After Jax died, there had been no gathering, no formality to mark the occasion. He had refused to hear of anything even remotely resembling a funeral, so those of us who had known him were denied any means of saying good-bye. Typical of him, I later thought but was too guilt-ridden to say.

"Oh yes, Jax. Of course I knew him well, as well as anyone did I would say," he said. "And Andrew of course, I suppose he told you about Andrew."

"Yes he did, and Andrew's book, very impressive," I said.

"Indeed, the book. A good many of my pieces in it."

He drummed his fingers once on the leather desktop.

"And did you say you worked together, you and Jax?" he asked.

"Yes, we did, at the antique shop downtown, well antiques and flowers, the one I just mentioned. I worked there and the owners are friends of mine," I said.

"I see, and tell me, at this antique shop, flower shop, just what did Jax do there?"

"He helped out, waited on customers for flowers, anything really," I said.

"Really," he said, as though I were saying something quite remarkable. "He did all that?"

"Yes sir," I answered.

I wasn't quite following him. Although I did not know this man at all, he did seem to have something on his mind.

"Willingly?" he asked.

"Uh, yes. It was his idea about the job in the first place. I mean, he asked me."

"Oh I'm sure that would have been the case, but that's not quite what I was getting at. No, I'm wondering about what he did there, really did there. At this shop, tell me truthfully, did you actually get any work out of our Jax?"

At this last question, he raised an eyebrow and looked me in the eye.

"Uh, he worked there a couple days a week," I said. What was he getting at?

"No, no, I mean did you get any work out of him?" he pressed. "Did he do anything whilst he was there?"

He tapped each word into the desktop with his index finger.

"Or did he sit around and do as little as one could think humanly possible?"

"Well, um," I stammered.

I was flummoxed. Just what was he saying? Was he insinuating what it sounded like he was insinuating?

Before I could go further, he threw his head back and let out a laugh.

"Just as I thought," he said. "He did sweet Fanny Adams, did he not?"

I stared at him with a look that betrayed my confusion.

"I'm sorry?" I asked.

I felt something akin to panic coming over me, but at the same time something else, an inkling, an understanding was beginning to dawn on me.

"He did nothing, was useless. You know it, but you're too polite to say so," he jeered, until he choked with laughter.

I felt the blood rushing to my face, indicating I was blushing, and I produced a weak smile that grew stronger by the moment.

"Now tell me it is not so," he insisted, continuing to laugh. "Oh I knew her well, Jaxie. She didn't like to work, she didn't. She was much better at fluttering those big brown eyes. That's what she was used to doing rather than turning her hand to doing a day's labour."

I guffawed in spite of myself.

"Yes, you're right, he used to work some for me here, if you can call it that. Mother of God, he used to irritate the bejesus out of me. Looking pretty, that was about all she was good for. Hoo, oh no, I'm sure your friends had their hands full trying to get him off his backside."

His face was positively red from laughing.

"Oh God rest her soul, silly Jaxie, daft cow that she was."

His expression was one of joy and of mirth. I could plainly see that he wasn't troubled in the least by what he had just said, which was brutal, wicked even, but completely without malice. And we both knew it was true, so very true.

I began to laugh. Oh god did I laugh. I laughed like someone possessed, like the prisoner who has just learned of the governor's pardon, like the shipwrecked who sees the rescue boat on the horizon, like the prophet who has had the scales fall from his eyes, like someone who has just had a great weight lifted off him, which I reckon, to be honest,

I just had. There was no shame in it. I laughed until I had to wipe my eyes, wiping away the first tears that I had shed for Jax. They were not the tears of guilt and remorse that I had sought, but the purifying tears of laughter. We were still snickering once I stood up from the elegant chair.

"Come by anytime," he said to me as he shook my hand and followed me to the door.

The sky was so very blue and the air so very crisp out on the pavement. As I walked back toward the East Village, I felt practically airborne. It reminded me of the liberating feeling I had when I sold all my belongings not long before. I wasn't quite sure what had just happened, but I had just come to realise that for the second time within a month, a good-natured antique dealer had taken all sort of old possessions, goods become encumbrances, off my hands.

Pigeon Under Glass

T he afternoons were the worst. They dragged on and on, until at times he wondered if somehow, someone was tampering with the time, by unknown means slowing it down, so that the hands on his watch were practically frozen in place, barely moving between the intervals in which he raised his sweaty wrist and looked down at the watch face. The shop was too warm, the air stagnant, due to the fact that the air conditioning was broken again. The system was ancient and far too costly for the company to replace. Customers would approach him, indignant in their discomfort.

"I simply can't see why you keep it so warm in here. It's ridiculous," they would say, using that tone of voice with which he was so familiar, that inflection that wealthy, entitled people employ when they complain.

"You really should do something about it. It is far too warm for us to shop," they would insist, as though he himself were personally culpable for their rapidly deteriorating retail experience.

The store was large and located in one of

London's wealthiest boroughs, opened back in the glory days of the company, when the well-connected, patrician owner was the last word in home fashion. He had vision, but that was nearly forty years ago, and the market and owners had changed. The company had since fallen on hard times, and the vast, white space was expensive to maintain. Now, walls went unpainted; cooling systems were not repaired. The furniture on display, all pale wood and white lacquer, in an ongoing endeavour to make it fresh and alluring to customers and their pocketbooks, was positioned and repositioned around the interior, dragged back and forth across the floors time and again, until the joints eventually loosened and it all, ultimately, fell apart. Enticing sofas and chairs, clad in crème fabric, that safe and neutral shade of middle England, grew grubby from the hordes of families flopping onto them, children standing on them, and babies being changed upon them. Every cushion was covered in rusk crumbs.

Then there was the ceaseless dirt, blowing in through the desperately beckoning open doors from the busy street outside, issuing from the belching exhaust pipes of countless buses and trendy sport utility vehicles, covering everything, settling onto the glass table tops and lacquer chests. Endless dusting only managed to grind it, black and gritty, into the wood surfaces and the moulded plastic chairs. It permanently tinted the clothing. Will's cheap black trousers and black polo shirt - the company required the wearing of black - both laundered time and again, in an attempt to wash out the filth, were gradually transformed into another colour altogether, more of a hazy grey than black.

The staff on the shop floor were getting sleepy in the warmth, their gaze becoming fixed, their eyelids starting to droop. Little chance of anyone coming in and buying a sofa in this environment. It was the worst combination, a slow afternoon with few customers and a hot, stagnant shop. They were practically dozing off while standing, and he continuously had to tell them off for yawning. Most of them were young and bright, more interested in socialising and partying than retail. The last thing they desired was being rooted to one spot all day in the vexing heat and being testily asked, "Why is there no lift?" They weren't delinquent or lazy, Will knew, just uninspired and well aware that the company saw them as little more than cheap labour, drones.

"Will, can I go on my break?" one of the boys asked him, forming a T-shaped, "time out" sign with his hands as he trotted to the stairs.

"Yes, go on, and don't be late coming back," Will answered, looking down at his watch to see what time the youth left.

You had to watch them like a hawk, or else they would sit up in the staff room, reclining on the tattered old sofas, long beyond their allotted break time.

"You lot are turning my hair grey," he would tease them in the morning meetings, something which had more than a ring of truth to it. His hair was indeed, as he could see in the mirror, like his shirt and trousers, slowly turning grey.

The afternoon sun streaming through the full-length windows was only adding to the heat. They ran across the entire front of the store, floor to ceiling, offering passers-by unobstructed views of the furniture room sets arranged inside. It was all positioned to catch the eye of passing trade, but it was difficult to say what those outside actually did see. He remembered that one day a woman had hopped off of the number twenty-two bus and mistaking a reflection for the entrance, ran smack into the glass. She sunk to the pavement, leaving a pink smear of frosted lipstick zigzagging down the face of the window.

"Blind old bat," one of the boys later guffawed, the laughter continuing for days afterward in the staff room. They took their amusement when and where they could find it.

Far easier to discern, from inside of the store, was the incessant activity unfolding on the high street. From his position behind the windows, Will could see the busy crowds outside on the pavement. They were well-dressed, purposeful, talking on mobiles, carrying shopping bags, pushing prams and push chairs. He envied them. He wasn't certain exactly what it was that he coveted in them, but he felt it tugging at his throat and belly nonetheless. Perhaps it was what he perceived as their freedom. If they came in and it was too warm for them, they of course could simply leave. What they never seemed to see was that he and the weary staff had no choice but to remain. He longed to remind some of the pampered, moaning customers of that, but being in the position that he was, he obviously could not. Customers never appreciated having the obvious pointed out to them.

He was a manager in the store, not the store manager or general manager, but a lesser one, something above the sales staff but certainly, clearly below the upper management. "All the responsibility but none of the authority," he liked to say. Often he was the first in in the morning and the last out in the evening. He did all of the grunt work, looking after the staff, dealing with customers, confronting drunks and shoplifters. "I see it all," he always said. The staff moaned to him about their rotas, about the store manager, and about the short-sighted, dehumanising directives issuing from head office, while the store manager took him to task over the dress and demeanour of the staff, the housekeeping, and of course the sales. He prided himself on his ability to keep both, if not happy, then at bay. However, the same could not be said of his relationship with the company's upper management.

He wasn't popular with any of them, no matter how he attempted to make a favourable impression. He always seemed to put a foot wrong, to say the wrong thing, to ask the wrong question. His regional manager, a brash, loud redhead with high heels and thick ankles who spoke estuary

English, had no use for him.

"Keep your eyes on the prize," she always quipped, as she stomped through the store, the cliché causing him to cringe inside. She liked her managers self-made, none too educated, more working class, like she herself was. Having none of these qualities, Will was not her type and thus, in her view, could do very little right.

If he dared mention the broken air conditioning, she spat back at him, "Stop being so negative."

He was going nowhere in the company and was well aware of the fact. It was as if he were standing before an invisible wall, a wall checking his movement, a wall which he ran into time after time, banging his head, knocking himself back, until he was too worn out to move.

"Could a manager please come to the main till," came the muffled sound from the tannoy. He took a deep breath at this. Being called to the till always filled him with trepidation. It was a minefield, as it oftentimes indicated trouble, usually in the form of an unhappy customer.

"Are you the manager?" they would begin.

"I'm one of them," he would say, "How can I help you?"

"Well, I bought this not more than a month ago, and I'm very disappointed. As you can see, it's not fit for purpose."

He would then be presented with some battered old object, a tea towel, a pan, looking for all the world like it had been dropped from a belfry or had been run over by a lorry, and he wondered how something could possibly have got into such a state. They would look him right in the eye, not blinking nor hesitating, and declare that they had just bought it, had not even used it, even though it was a decade old if it were a day. He would have to hide the look that would involuntarily come across his face, that pained look of enduring the presence of unashamed, bold-faced mendacity. *Not fit for purpose:* he pondered where they picked up this sort of language.

Once he had a woman throw a wok at him.

"My ninety year old mother could have been killed," she screamed, the faint odour of vintage chardonnay wafting on her breath. "It's not properly designed. Even you can see that."

She had not put the handle on, he noticed later, only after she had stormed out of the store in a blind rage, her expensive shoes clattering on the terrazzo floor. He loved how she had felt the necessity to add, "even you" to her attack. The wealthy ones could be the worst. For all their airs and graces, they could turn on you at a moment's notice, tearing into you with a ferocity which was matched only by their condescension.

For the present however, it was only a refund he had to authorise. He stepped behind the worn counter, its grey, plastic laminate chipped and in need of refurbishment, to the till where his member of staff, a pleasant Polish girl named Alicja, had beckoned him.

"Can you authorise this please? It's above my

limit," she said.

He looked up at the customer standing across the counter, a tall man wearing shorts and a polo shirt, and said, "Hello."

"Hi," the man answered, looking amiably at him.

Oftentimes they simply looked right through you, not bothering to acknowledge your presence in the least. While he perfunctorily tapped the required code into in the till, he felt the man's gaze remain fixed upon him. Sometimes they would stare at you for no reason.

"And that's done for you," Will said, glancing up.

"Thanks," the man said, then added, "I see there are no pigeons today."

"I'm sorry?"

Will gave him a perplexed look.

"I see there aren't any pigeons. You're the one who caught the pigeon aren't you?" he said. "I couldn't tell if it was you or not, but you are the one."

"Pigeon?"

"That's right. I was here that day when you caught the pigeon."

Will was taken aback, slightly confused. Then it all came back to him, the pigeon.

"Oh yeah, I had forgotten about that, that pigeon," Will said.

"I think it had wandered into the store or something, and I remember seeing you."

"Wow, that was a while ago. Maybe a year or

more?"

"Yes, I think it could have been. That was really something."

Will had completely forgotten about it. It had all transpired in just a few minutes, and as soon as it happened, it was over. How strange that someone, a stranger, a person he did not even know, had never met, should remember it. Even more remarkable perhaps is that this man not only should remember the incident but also remembered him.

It was an afternoon, not unlike this one, slow and boring, with few customers about. He was back in the stock room, fluorescent tube stuttering above his head, attempting to sort out some endless snarl in the inventory of some wine glasses, when one of his staff, Zoe, a thin, wan redhead and a vegetarian if he remembered correctly, came running in, distraught and out of breath.

"Will, Will, come quick, we need you," she shouted.

"What?" he answered, annoyed at being interrupted mid-count. "What is it, honey?"

"You've got to come out. There's a bird in the store."

"A what?" he asked turning around. He noticed that she was sporting black-painted fingernails and wondered if they adhered to dress code.

"A bird, a pigeon. It's in the store."

"Well shoo it outside for goodness sake," he said.

"We can't. It keeps flying into the window. Ooh it's awful. You've got to come and do something." She whining like a child.

"Oh for pity sake, " he said putting down his clipboard with some resignation.

He left the stockroom and followed Zoe out on to the shop floor, past the sofas, chairs and tables to the front of the store where the staff were all gathered near the front windows. They had formed a kind of semi-circle, a semi-circle of faded grey-black uniforms. As they saw him approaching, they began to point at the window.

"Will, it's a pigeon. It's a pigeon," they shouted in chorus.

"So I gather," he said in a deadpan voice. "So why haven't you taken him outside?"

"No way," someone answered. "Oh no, it keeps flying and crashing into the window."

"Ew, it's over there," Zoe whimpered, pointing with her black-nailed hand.

"Oh don't be so silly," Will said in mock disdain, suppressing a smile.

Now that he was out of the stockroom, he was glad of the diversion actually. The circle opened up before him with the staff standing aside as he approached. There, some distance away, huddled on the floor against one of the windows was a bird, feathers slightly ruffled, in shades of grey and black, a pigeon, a pigeon identical to the numberless ones you see all over London. It looked small, fragile, of no account, and out of place. In the crème and white of the store interior, it definitely looked out of place. Furthermore, it did not move, which lead Will to wonder if it were even alive.

"What are you going to do?" someone whined.

"Well we've got to get it out of here, don't we?" he said.

"But how? It keeps crashing into the window."

Of course, he had no idea what was to be done. He stepped within the circle toward the window where the bird stood frozen, its red eyes blinking from time to time. He took a few paces, stopped, then took a few more. When he got to within twelve feet or so, the bird suddenly leapt into life. Flapping its wings wildly, it slammed itself repeatedly into the window glass. It made a terrible rhythmic, thrashing sound accompanied by desperate cooing.

Zoe screamed, "Oh shit."

"Shut up," Will said turning in her direction and giving her a look, "Good god, what is wrong with you?"

Unable to go anywhere, the pigeon soon slowed its thrashing and again perched on the floor against the window. It was clearly exhausted. Will stood still until it settled, noticing the iridescent green colouring of its neck. Exhaustion was something he knew from experience.

He once had a cat, a pedigreed oriental shorthair, that was constantly bringing birds into the flat. Other cats, those of no particular breed, would look on passively at birds, but this particular cat was ferocious, and he thought it was interesting that the most well-bread, the most refined breeds, oftentimes were the most vicious. You would think that it would have been bred out of them. Even the large wood pigeons would this cat stalk, attack, and stuff through the cat flap, and which Will would have to capture and turn loose. Once the bird became too weary to attempt to fly away, he learned, it was an easy thing to catch and dispose of.

He slowly circled round to the right, not getting any closer to the pigeon, but positioning himself to where the bird's head was facing away. Once he had got himself directly behind, and thus out of its line of sight, he noiselessly, smoothly moved toward it, bending over as he did so. The pigeon did not move, remaining crouched down against the window. Will could just make out a blinking red eye. Then ever so carefully, he reached his hands out and placed them around the bird. Neither struggling nor attempting to fly away, it only jerked its head to one side and opened its beak as though asking, "Who?"

"Oh my god," someone shouted.

With the pigeon safely held in both hands before him, like a drinks tray full of glasses, Will stood up and smiled.

"Nothing to it," he said and laughed, clearly pleased with himself.

He was amazed at how little it weighed, like carrying a pin cushion, albeit a pin cushion with a wildly beating heart somewhere within it. The pigeon only blinked blankly. Will walked toward the open door carrying it, the circling crowd of staff and by this time, curious onlookers parting before him.

Once outside on the pavement, he paused for a moment, looking up toward the afternoon sun. Then swinging his outstretched arms into the air, lifting the pigeon, he separated his hands outwards, and the inanimate bird at once opened its wings and flapped into the air. After flying a few yards, it quietly, languidly landed on the pavement, blinked, and pecked at a cigarette butt. Will mimed a stage frown and shook his head as though disappointed in the bird's apparent lack of afflatus.

"Well, you got out dumbass," he said somewhat darkly.

Then turning, he brushed his hands together; they were covered with a sooty, black dust. As he walked back inside the store, he was greeted with a cheer from the staff.

"Did you see that?" someone shouted.

They were all giddy, cheery with excitement and in a happy mood. Everyone laughed; they took their amusement when and where they could find it.

As Alicja entered the card details into the till, Will stood beside her, listening to the customer, the tall man.

"I remember you walked over, you scooped it up, and you took it outside, and then you just let it go, and it flew away," the man said. "I guess I remember it because it's not something you see every day, someone just walking over and picking up a pigeon and setting it free just like that. I mean, I wonder what would have happened? I guess it would have been stood there butting its head up against the glass forever."

"I suppose so," Will said as the man was turning to leave.

He stepped from behind the till and gradually made his way back across the sales floor, toward the front of the store. He walked up to the vast, sweltering expanse of window, stopped and paused, peering out. The sun was setting, the red monolithic forms of the slow, ponderous buses casting shadows on the pavement outside. People were walking by, looking purposeful, busy, and contented. They all certainly looked as though they had someplace to go, as though they knew where they were headed.

"Yeah, I guess forever," Will said to himself in the direction of the glass, and raising his sweaty wrist, looked at his watch.

Transport For London

I t all started out so innocently. I stepped out of the club a little unsteadily, and passing the doorman, I was thrust full on into the cool night air. The wet vapour and warm smoke of the inside was belching out of the doorway behind me like something from an industrial chimney. My ears were ringing after spending so much time on the dance floor with the booming, throbbing music, which made the outside, by contrast, seem hushed. As I stood on the pavement in front of the club for a moment to gain my bearings, the traffic of Vauxhall speeded past nearby.

I had had a bit too much to drink and had done a few too many bumps of K, the preferred, gay, party drug at the time. It was necessary to get some fresh air to clear my head, and then I needed to get home, as it was Sunday night, and it was late. Chatting and laughing in pairs and in groups, the clubbers stood about in the space between the tottering pile of the Tavern and the looming bulk of the railway arches. Up above, beside the train tracks, an illuminated billboard glowed like some sort of urban moon. I shivered slightly, although it was not really cold, just so much cooler than it had been inside, where it was hot and steamy, everyone with their shirts off and dancing. My jeans felt damp.

"Right," I said to myself (and to anyone else whom I thought might be within earshot), "First of all, what time is it, and what day is it?" This was Vera's famous line from *Auntie Mame*, which I repeated whenever I deemed appropriate, and now seemed as an appropriate time as any other. I, like Vera who suddenly found herself, confused and blinking, thrust into the outside world, was discovering myself to be not quite *en pointe*. Shaking my head rapidly back and forth, as if I were attempting to fling some noisome, rattling pebbles out of it, I dizzily headed for the road crossing.

There, the light turned green, traffic halted momentarily, and I carefully forayed across the vast canyon of South Lambeth Road.

"The Tube, I need the Tube," I said to myself, picking up speed as I scuttled across the wide expanse of roadway. My steps however, seemed a bit stilted, as though I were prancing like a horse.

You've done this a thousand times; there's nothing to it, I reassured myself, bombarded by the echoes bouncing about the pedestrian tunnel through which I passed, the K still coursing through my brain, distorting and somehow amplifying the din, and yet making it all seem far away.

The more I walked, I could not help but notice that my feet felt strange, a sensation that I could only describe as if they were somehow made of marshmallows. This was another effect of the drug, I knew from experience. A few moments later, I made my way down the station steps into the noisy ticket hall and proceeded through the turnstile as nonchalantly as I could muster, then hopped, a little unsteadily, onto the crowded escalator leading down to the tracks. Once reaching the bottom, and looking right through the openings - I suppose I was drawn to that sound familiar to all Tube commuters, the comforting purr of the idling electric motor of the Tube train, the reassuring indicator that it is at the station and available for embarkation - I spotted a coach stopped at the platform, beckoning, with its doors open.

Instinctively, I ran for it, just as I heard the announcement, *"Please mind the closing doors."* I leapt into the coach just as the warning beeper sounded and the doors rolled shut conclusively behind me.

Yes! I thought in triumph, smiling to myself. I do love it when I am able to catch the Tube without having to wait. Now, all I had to do was go two stops up to Victoria, change for the District Line, and I was practically home. The coach was full, mostly young people, loud and pissed, coming home from pubs and clubs. They dangled perilously from the overhead straps when the train pulled away from the platform, and they shouted animatedly in each other's flushed faces. The light in the coach, for my eyes, appeared to be rather bluish, and unnaturally bright.

The train had picked up speed through the

tunnel, then slowed, when I heard the announcement, sounding as though it were emanating from some far distant source, *"The next station is Stockwell. Alight here for the Northern Line."*

I remained motionless, it taking a moment in my altered state to take in what the announcement had actually said; then my breathing stopped short.

What? I thought, *"Stockwell? Stockwell? That's not right. It should be...it should be Pimlico.*

Something was amiss. How was it that I was in Stockwell? My mind swirled in confusion and I had a momentary attack of panic. Trying my hardest to make my muddled, floating head work, I concentrated as much as I could muster. Then slowly, I came to the realisation that I somehow must have got onto the southbound rather than the northbound train. How had I done that?

Oh shit, I thought.

What was I going to do? All I knew was that I was approaching Brixton, the end of the line, and in the opposite direction of where I wanted to be or to go. It seemed to take forever, arriving to the next station, the train whining loudly as it slowed down. When it finally stopped and the doors opened with a dry hiss, I leapt off in order to figure out just what my next move should be. I took a deep breath and pondered for a moment, trying my damnedest to brush the hazy cobwebs from my mind.

After a moment of what seemed like the most intense exercising of my brain, I managed to come up with a solution.

Ah, all you have to do is go across the platform and

get the next train back, and then you'll be fine. Don't panic, I reassured myself.

And just at that moment, as if on cue, a train pulled up to the platform opposite.

Great, I thought, *catastrophe averted*.

I decisively made my way across the platform, boarded this train, and gave a sigh of relief as the doors shut and it speeded off.

I was beginning to calm down and was starting to make light of my silly drug-addled mistake.

Then I heard the announcement, *"The next station is Clapham North."*

A shock ran through me as though I had touched a faulty kettle.

Clapham North? Clapham North?

Clapham North was rolling, practically shouting through my brain. I didn't even know where Clapham North was.

How have I done this? I asked.

For the second time in as many minutes, I anxiously awaited for the next stop as waves of panic swept over me. This was getting serious.

I looked up and attempted to read the small Tube map overhead, but to no avail. The combination of dance floor smoke, drugs, and my insistence on wearing contact lenses that no longer even remotely corrected my vision, made the prospect of deciphering the map about as likely as my decoding Linear A. All I could make out was an advert placed in the frieze that ran overhead. In bold black letters, it began, "LIFE'S A JOURNEY...," the rest of it too small for me to make out.

As I had done only a few minutes before, I leapt off of the train as soon as the doors opened. I marched over to the large Tube map mounted in the middle of the platform, squinting my eyes in a most unbecoming fashion in an attempt to decipher the colourful, spaghetti-like maze of lines. It appeared that rather than returning to Vauxhall on the Victoria line, I had somehow boarded a southbound Northern Line train by mistake.

Never, never again try to get home on the Tube after doing K, I chided myself.

Now, I needed to take another train back to Stockwell in order to start my northward journey all over again. I ran up the steps and dizzily looked about for the correct platform. The tunnel was full of people making their way out, shouting and carrying tins of cider.

Why does there always seem to be a girl named Gemma who is lost or lagging behind, I thought, *so that her mates have to repeatedly shout her name, over and over?*

Finally, in my urgency, I spotted the northbound platform, trotted nervously down the stairs, and planted myself there to await the next train. I looked up at the electronic board, but all I could make out through my filmy vision was, "NO SMOKING," blinking periodically.

"Come on," I said aloud, kicking myself inside.

I looked around, and there was only one other person on the platform, a rather plump, youngish man wearing Peter Pan boots with his trouser legs tucked into them. I was beginning to worry, as I now knew that I had a great deal of ground to cover in order to correct my mistakes and to eventually get home. I waited another few minutes, wishing beyond words for the train to arrive. Then, through the muddiness in my head it slowly dawned on me that I was hearing something, something far away.

I cocked my ear instinctively, when I heard it again, a voice, a voice shouting, "Hello...hello."

I spun around, startled, and looked up, and was just able to make out the form of a uniformed man standing over on the stairs.

"Hello," he repeated, "the station is closed."

"What?" I heard the other man on the platform, the plump one shout.

"There are no more trains, mate," the station attendant said. "The last train just left. You need to leave."

"Oh shit," I said to myself, and stood frozen to the spot.

"You need to leave, now," the attendant repeated, seeing that neither I nor the plump guy were moving.

With that, after a huge exhale like a balloon let loose, I dejectedly headed in his direction, his retreating figure quickly disappearing as I slowly walked up the steps and to the escalator. The man in the boots followed behind me, becoming more and more agitated as it became clear just what was going on, that the trains were finished for the night.

"Oh my god, what am I supposed to do?" he

shouted as we ascended the escalator. "Last train? What *is* that? What *is* he talking about?"

I noticed that he was wearing a sparkly, blowsy t-shirt with the word, "Sexy" floridly printed on it in glitter. It clung damply and rather unflatteringly to his bulging midriff. As we reached the exit, I saw the attendant who had just spoken to us earlier, stationed there with one hand placed authoritatively on the metal shutters, utter blackness of the outside beyond him.

"Are there no more trains?" Sexy shouted. His face and neck were sweaty-looking.

"No mate," the attendant said, "you missed the last train."

"Oh my god, how am I supposed to get home?" he asked, becoming more hysterical by the second.

I noticed a tuft of dark, damp hair peeping out of the neck of his tee shirt, looking none too attractive against his pale skin.

"Don't know mate. You can get a night bus." No doubt he repeated this same line on a nightly basis.

"But I'm going to Colliers Wood. Is there a bus to Colliers Wood from here?" Sexy demanded.

"Don't know mate, you'll have to look out at the bus stop. To your left."

I hadn't said anything up to this point, partly because I was worried whether I could be coherent, and partly because I knew, coherent or not, that arguing with the bloke at the station, no doubt a union man, was not going to get me home.

I passed by him, the attendant, saying only, "Good night."

Sexy, however, stopped to plead with him a moment longer.

"This is not funny," he whined. "I don't have any more money," he added.

The attendant, obviously used to this, was unmoved, uttering only monosyllables in response. Eventually, at the very second that Sexy gave up and finally passed over the threshold to the outside, the attendant quickly slammed the shutters closed behind him and deftly locked them. I turned around to look, and he had already disappeared from view within the station. Sexy and I were alone, all alone outside of the station.

"How are you getting home?" Sexy asked, suddenly turning his attentions on me.

His hair was long in the back and high - it appeared to be backcombed - in the front. A moustache was squeezed into the space between his chubby cheeks.

"I don't know." I said, "I'm not sure I know where I am exactly." Looking around into what looked to be intense darkness, I said, "Get a cab I guess."

Sexy jumped on this. "Oh a cab, fab. Do you think you could drop me off on your way?"

"I don't know. Maybe," I said. "Where are you going?"

"Colliers Wood," he said. Then he added, as nonchalantly as he could muster, "But now see, the only problem is, I don't have any money. So could you could just drop me off on your way?"

"Colliers Wood?" I said, "Where is that exactly? Isn't that south of here? See, I'm going north to Chelsea. I think that would be way out of my way."

"Oh it's not far, really," he said, dismissing with a florid flick of his thick wrist the fact the he wanted to go almost to Zone Four. "I don't have any money and I don't have any other way to get back. So you can just drop me off on your way home. It's easy."

At that his mobile rang. He pulled out a handset with a rhinestone-bedecked cover and launched into a dramatic recitation of his current woes to whoever was on the other end.

"You're not going to believe what's happened," he shouted, "Only they've gone and stopped the trains before I could get home."

He turned and paced in the opposite direction, engrossed in regaling the person on the other end with the indignities heaped upon him by Transport For London.

Left to myself, I scanned the immediate area around the station in an attempt to see if I recognised anything. When I thought of Clapham, its busy high street came to mind, with its packed bars and restaurants. I couldn't see any of that here. It appeared all deserted and darkness. There were two forlorn little roads to my right, a train bridge blocking the view to my left, and the road climbing bleakly uphill straight ahead of me.

I pulled out my wallet and peeked inside.

There was a lone, twenty-pound note. That would get me home in a cab, I reasoned, but would certainly not stretch to a midnight jaunt down south and then back north across the river. There was no way. I hardly knew where I was now, much less where this Sexy wanted to go, but I was sure that twenty pounds would not be sufficient. I saw him over in the distance, illuminated by the street light, his free hand flailing as an accompaniment to his speaking.

"Yeah, yeah, there's someone who's sharing a cab with me," I overheard him saying in the distance.

What have I got myself into? I thought, looking out into the dark. *I'm glad that he just naturally assumed that I would take him where ever it is he is going to....and pay for it,* I mused.

However, at any rate, whatever he assumed, I knew that I did not have enough money. Therefore, something was going to have to give.

"What a nightmare this has all turned into," I said to myself, becoming mildly exasperated. "If you hadn't taken the wrong Tube, none of this would be happening."

Sexy was in the distance still on the mobile, and I could just overhear him saying, "I told Stacy that I don't talk to people I don't know already, and if Lee was going to act like a b-i-t-c-h, then I was going to leave."

I peered out into the road that disappeared over the dismal hill, wondering what I was going to do.

Then, suddenly, I saw a light. It took a second for me to determine whether this was simply a flickering hallucination in my drug-fuzzy head or something actual and external. Appearing at the crest of the dark hill, it hovered, allowing me the time to process that it was not some lingering bit of party-K but real and verifiable illumination. The familiar beacon of an amber light had appeared out of the blackness, and now was making its way slowly down the hill in my direction.

How do I convey the exhilaration that you experience when you see that most welcome of indicators of a free black cab, that burning yellow radiance slicing through the darkness? My feeling is that it could only be compared to what must certainly be the almost overwhelming joy of the shipwrecked when they, at long last, spot the rescue boat. As it approached, I was greeted by that particular sound peculiar to London black cabs, a ticking, stuttering hum, more akin to an industrial sewing machine than an internal combustion engine.

I threw up my arm and ran out into the turning of the side road fronting the station, waving frantically the entire time. The cab responded in kind by producing a quick flicker of its headlights. As it slowed and then halted before me, I quickly turned and looked back toward the station. Sexy was still there off in the distance, chattering away, oblivious to me, oblivious to the light.

"I don't know why she done them shots," I could just hear him saying.

I paused for a moment, but only a split moment, then spun around and loped up to the window of the cab, my feet still a bit marshmallowy.

I said to the driver, "Chelsea please," and as he nodded in the affirmative, I opened the back door and scrambled as noiselessly as I could into the spacious, grey interior.

It was only when I slammed the door closed that Sexy turned around, mobile still clamped to his ear. He started in surprise, his mouth suddenly gaping open, and letting the hand holding the mobile drop from his ear, his other hand pointed in my direction with a fat, sausage-like finger. Then, for the second time since I had made his acquaintance that evening, Sexy suddenly had a flash of realisation. He tore off with an ungainly dash in the direction of the cab, his Peter Pan boots slapping clumsily on the pavement.

"Hey, wait for me," he screamed. "Where are you going? You're supposed to drop me off."

"Drive," I said to the cabby, my manner suddenly becoming quite authoritative.

Without hesitation, he accelerated, the cab circling sharply into the main road and throwing me back against the seat in the process. Without my having to ask, he automatically locked the doors as we passed by the Tube station, speeding right by the bewildered, breathless Sexy. The glittery shirt sparkled gaily in the half light as he stood there panting and sweating.

I could hear his voice, from out in the middle

of the road, fading behind me, "Come back. Come back. How am I supposed to get home?"

I glanced into the driver's mirror and could see him watching the receding spectacle. He said nothing.

As we passed under the rail bridge, I came to realise that we were on Clapham High Street, had been on Clapham High Street all along. I knew where I was, and perhaps it was the last residue of the K, but the lights seemed glowing and festive.

Resisting the urge to turn and look back again, I spoke up, saying, "Oh my."

"That your mate?" the driver asked.

"I don't even know him," I said. "He missed the last train and wanted me to drop him off at Colliers Wood on my way home to Chelsea."

"He's having a laugh," the driver said, looking at me through his mirror.

"You're telling me. I mean, there is a limit," I said, turning my gaze toward the window beside me.

Then, after peering out into the comforting lights of Clapham High Street for a moment, I added, "It seems like some people are always off on the wrong track."

The Queen's Park

At long last and much to her own relief, Mary Helen Hager had just spotted the gift shop at Windsor Castle. In recognition of this achievement, she paused a moment on the slope to readjust her heavy quilted handbag with the gold-chain trimming, and to push her rimless glasses up a bit further on her nose. The shop was contained within a small, cobbled courtyard with a portable ice cream stand to one side. That is how it had all started, the idea of the vacation, months ago, with the mention of the gift shop at the Queen's residence of all things. It was during the party at her neighbour Linda Lee Bumgarner's house last Christmas - they were in Junior League together - and she had seen those gorgeous little Christmas ornaments on her tree, which everybody was just going on and on about.

Those Christmas ornaments were stunning, handmade and all embroidered with silver, gold, coloured threads, beads, and sequins. They depicted various quaint, English things: a Tudor rose, an antique cross, a soldier with bearskin hat, Henry VIII, and perhaps cutest of all, the Queen's crown. Of course, when Mary Helen Hager had remarked on them, Linda Lee Bumgarner, who lives three doors down at one-fifteen, had mentioned casually that she and her husband Raymond had, "picked them up" at Windsor Castle, on their last trip to England.

It was at that moment that Margaret Burke Ragsdale piped up and remarked, "You know what, I think we should go over there to England, and we can buy us some of those darling little geegaws as well." Margaret Burke Ragsdale was Mary Helen Hager's best friend. They had known each other from their childhood in the neighbourhood, attending First Presbyterian Church as well as John McKnitt Alexander High School together. They had both been bridesmaids in each other's wedding.

That is how it had all started; that day at Linda Lee Bumgarner's the plan was hatched, and from there, it had developed into a full-blown itinerary of a vacation to Britain for the Hagers and the Ragsdales. They would go to England in the summer, which would be educational and a nice change, making certain to visit Windsor Castle along the way. While she probably would never have come up with the idea of of this vacation herself, Mary Helen Hager had always been interested, she reassured herself, in the sites and history of England, and she was certainly keen to see where the Queen lived. Obviously, it went without saying, that she would be happy to purchase some of those cute little Christmas ornaments while she was there as well.

The trip was nothing if not nice, beginning in the north and working its way southward, but to be honest, Mary Helen Hager was as busy considering just what their return home would bring in the form of enhanced social life, as she was taking in the sights. She was beside herself thinking about how people would be making over their vacation, not to mention her Christmas tree, just like they had been at Linda Lee Bumgarner's last year.

She could not help but see herself, dressed in a festive Christmas sweater, cup of fragrant mulled wine in hand, addressing the assembled neighbours.

"Aren't those adorable?" she would begin. "We came across those at Windsor Castle last summer when we were in England. You know, they have some of the quaintest customs over there. We met some actual English, and they told us how the Scottish people and the English people don't get along with each other. Can you imagine that, living practically on each other's doorstep on such a teeny little island to begin with, and they can't get along?"

This last bit she had learned, only a few days into the trip, after being corrected by a dour Scots tour guide whom she had insulted by addressing him as English.

"I thought you were all English," she said in dismay.

He had responded by calling her a "wee daft bat," whatever that was.

Mary Helen Hager had never been out of the

country before, except for that time they took that cruise to the Bahamas. This trip was quite a change from their usual vacation at Hilton Head, which she always enjoyed, because she felt it was always their sort of people there. With the exception of some of the Yankees, who always seemed to talk way too loud and would try to push in front of you at the Whole Foods, the island was always visited by people much the same as them, which was a good thing surely.

It wasn't that she had any problem with foreign types and what not, far from it. Mary Helen Hager felt that one of her strong suits was her ability to meet people from all walks of life. She reminded herself about the time that she had hosted a reception for that group of Christian singers from Scandinavia who were visiting First Presbyterian, even going so far as to put fresh dill in her potato salad. Everyone was so impressed at how she had gone to all that trouble and made them all feel so welcome in Middlesboro. Even so, and those singers were just as nice as they could be, but because they were from so far away, they were always going to be, well, different. Say what you will, but Mary Helen Hager had always prided herself on knowing what was what, and the indisputable fact of the matter, as she was simply all too aware, is that you will always have more in common with people from your own neck of the woods.

The gift shop in the Castle precinct lay just ahead, discreetly placed within some old buildings, its entry through a low, wide stone arch adorned with a pair of topiaries. A tasteful sign announced its presence. Both couples had spent all morning taking in the voluptuous state rooms of the castle, and while she had to say that she certainly enjoyed viewing with the others, one regal interior after another regal interior crammed with vases, chandeliers, and ponderous gilded furniture, wondering all the while just how they kept it all vacuumed and dusted, May Helen Hager was now happy to give herself a moment to herself, especially after Margaret Burke Ragsdale had embarrassed her half to death when she asked one of the guides why they had built the castle so close to the airport. Besides - and this had been in her mind all along - she wanted to get to the gift shop ahead of her best friend.

In anticipation, she picked up speed on the descent from the castle, her white walking shoes, bought especially for the trip, padding quietly over the gravel paving.

"Come on slowpoke," she turned and called out to Wendell her husband.

He was lagging behind, having just held up an entire tour of French people, much to Mary Helen Hager's irritation, by loitering in one of the narrow entryways taking a photograph. Like his wife, he was wearing no-iron, khaki shorts and an almost identical pair of walking shoes to hers, but in a men's version. An Indiana Jones type of hat, "for all the rain they have over there," had been firmly perched on his head for the entire trip, something which Mary Helen Hager had initially thought was cute but had gotten fed up with by the time they had reached York.

As she was about to cross the threshold of the shop, Wendell said to her, "There's a church or something down here that we've got to see yet."

"That's fine," she said, "but I'm going in here first."

At this, she stepped inside, her bright green raincoat suddenly disappearing from view, leaving Wendell to follow her in.

The gift shop was tastefully arranged with shelves on the perimeter walls neatly stacked with tins of tea, colourful scarves, embroidered cushions, and pastel-tinted china teapots and commemorative plates. Mary Helen Hager, ever the seasoned shopper, assumed that casual yet determined gait as she penetrated the depths of the shop. She turned her head first to the left, then to the right, putting on an air of complete nonchalance, belying the fact that she was definitely in search of something. She passed by, her eyes not lingering on, silver jewellery, mini tapestries, and jars of strawberry preserves, apparently made from strawberries from the Queen's own garden. Baskets piled full of cheap key rings and pencil sharpeners in the shape of a crown didn't even merit a second look.

At last, her gaze fell upon something which caught her attention. Along one wall, was a display of brightly hued little objects, no bigger than the palm of your hand, hanging via gold threads from horizontal rods projecting from the showcase. She walked toward them, and as she got nearer, she could just make out the various shapes: a cross, a crown, a stylised rose, and human figures in old-fashioned garb. As she approached, she also noticed standing there before the display case, a couple, woman and man, the man wearing an Indiana Jones hat on his head, the woman in a bright pink rain coat, khaki shorts, and white walking shoes. As Mary Helen Hager came to stand just to the right of the display, she was confirmed in her hunch that these were indeed the Christmas ornaments, right here before her, that Linda Lee Bumgarner had displayed on her tree. Awed by the dazzling array, she reached for the one dangling nearest to her, a likeness of Anne Boleyn, with head still attached, and lifted it off of the display hook. Yes, these were the ones, she thought to herself, holding up the gold-stitched effigy of Henry's ill-fated second wife, and giving herself a little smile of satisfaction, as she squinted in an attempt to make out the price.

Even in her delight, she could not help but notice the couple who were still standing next to her, the woman in the pink raincoat wearing a pleasant, toothy smile, admiring the very same objects that she herself was appraising. Now Mary Helen Hager was fully aware that in some parts of the world, like up North where they didn't have any manners, that people would stand right on top of each other and not speak, without even so much as a bye your leave, but that was certainly not the way they did things in North Carolina, except for maybe in Charlotte, but that spoke for itself.

Armed with this largess of Southern hospitality, she turned to the couple, smiled and held Anne Boleyn gaily aloft, saying, "Aren't these are just precious."

The woman in the pink raincoat perked up and managed to smile even more than she had been previously.

"I was just telling my husband that I want to take every one of these home with me," she beamed.

"Oh I know," Mary Helen Hager answered, "I could just eat them up. Aren't they the most darling things you've ever seen in your life?"

"They are," the other woman drawled. "They are sure going to make somebody's Christmas tree."

"Oh they are; they certainly are," Mary Helen Hager said with a broad smile. "The folks back home aren't going to know what to make of them."

After a moment, staring wide-eyed, the woman said, "You sound like you're from America?"

"I am from America," Mary Helen Hager answered in her most enthusiastic, patriotic, Junior League voice.

"So are we," the other woman enthused, matching Mary Helen Hager's ardour.

Her husband grinned from underneath the Indiana Jones hat.

"Isn't that something!" Mary Helen Hager

said. "Where in American are y'all from?"

"We're from North Carolina," the woman said, her excitement mimicking Mary Helen Hager's word for word.

"Really!" said Mary Helen Hager, "*We're* from North Carolina."

The woman's eyes grew round with this and she turned to the Indiana Jones hat in astonishment.

"Isn't that just too funny?" she said.

The man grinned, shaking the hat back and forth to indicate the sheer unlikelihood of such a thing ever happening.

At this point, their pleasantries were interrupted by the arrival of a short, dark-haired woman who pushed right through them in order to reach the ornaments. She was encased in what would seem to be a rather inappropriately heavy coat for the time of year, and she managed to bump into both the couple and Mary Helen Hager with her luridly patterned shoulder bag as she squeezed by. She grabbed an ornament from the off a hook, then spun around, shouting, staccato-fashion, across the gift shop, and into the faces of the stunned North Carolinians, in a language that none of them recognised. Getting no response, she shouted again, even more loudly. Mary Helen Hager and the couple eyed each other, lips pursed, without saying anything. A response in the same language, equally as loud, came from the other side of the shop, and the woman, with her large, rhinestone-bedecked sunglasses pushed back, brusquely, between the three again, as quickly as she had arrived, leaving them standing there a bit awestruck.

"Well let me just move out of your way, please ma'am," Mary Helen Hager declared with a flourish of her arm, after the woman was safely out of earshot.

"Well isn't that the truth?" the toothy woman said.

Mary Helen Hager continued, "I don't mean to be ugly, but some people just don't seem to have any manners whatsoever. I don't know where she is from, but don't they teach anybody anything there? One thing this vacation has shown me all too well is just how much I take for granted that most everybody back home knows how to behave."

The toothy woman nodded in agreement.

"I declare that is the gospel truth, things we don't even think about," she said. "I guess it takes us going somewhere else to make us see what all we have in common."

"You've got that right, yes siree, to see it and to appreciate it too," Mary Helen Hager continued, now well and truly engrossed in the proceedings.

She then let out a hearty laugh, to make it known that she was moving the conversation along.

"And speaking of home, now where did you say y'all are from in North Carolina, darling?" she asked.

"We're from Middlesboro," the woman said beaming at her husband as though this were something truly remarkable.

1

Mary Helen Hager squealed, launching into her best Southern woman's histrionics.

"No," she exclaimed.

She put both hands on her hips, while still keeping hold of Anne Boleyn.

"You're not going to believe this," she said, "but *we're* from Middlesboro too."

"Oh my goodness," the woman shouted, clasping her pearl necklace and gasping for breath. "Can you believe that Larry? They're from Middlesboro."

Her husband nodded the Indiana Jones hat in response.

Then catching herself, she exclaimed, "Lord, where are my manners? I'm just like a chicken with its head cut off. My name is Nancy Tarleton, and this is my husband Larry."

Mary Helen Hager was charmingly luminous.

"Well how do you do Nancy and Larry? So nice to meet you," she trilled in that well-practiced, high-pitched, Southern woman's wail. "I'm Mary Helen Hager, and..." at this she turned convulsively, searching for something and shouted across the shop, "Wendell, get over here. I've just met some folks from home."

She turned back to the couple and continued, "And on his way over here is my husband Wendell. Lord have mercy, I just might have to hug your neck."

The two women, giddy with laughter, politely embraced each other, like cousins who were meeting for the first time.

As Wendell came lumbering up, Mary Helen Hager said, "Honey, these are the Tarletons, Nancy and Larry. They're from Middlesboro."

The two women again broke into peals of laughter, while the pair of Indiana Jones hats shook hands with each other and grinned.

"It's just so nice to meet people from back home," Nancy Tarleton said.

"Oh I know," Mary Helen Hager agreed. "It's the nicest thing. You can go round the world, and I have met people from all over America and even other places, but there's nothing like people from your own home. My mother used to say that there's nothing like just good old folks."

"That is so true," Nancy Tarleton said with all the gravity of someone who has just had Scripture recited to them. "My mother used to say the very same thing."

The fact that neither mother had ever said anything even remotely like that was not really important at the moment.

"And here we ran into each other looking at these precious Christmas ornaments," she continued.

"Well," said Mary Helen Hager, "that just shows what good taste people from Middlesboro have, I reckon. I knew that the minute I saw you."

Nancy Tarleton threw her head back and laughed.

"I guess so," she giggled.

"Well this is really something," Mary Helen Hager said.

"Now where do y'all live in Middlesboro?" she asked.

"We live on Queen's Park Road," Nancy Tarleton said.

Mary Helen Hager's mouth fell open.

"No! I just don't believe it," she gushed, hardly able to contain herself. "Did you hear that Wendell? They live on Queen's Park Road," she bellowed at him, just in case he had not heard.

She then placed her hand on Nancy Tarleton's arm to prepare her for the next in what was becoming a most remarkable string of revelations.

"Now, you're not going to believe this," she shouted, "but *we* live on Queen's Park Road."

"No!" Nancy Tarleton shrieked. "Y'all live on Queen's Park Road too?"

"Yes we do, child," said Mary Helen Hager, tugging at her pearl necklace with the one hand and gripping Nancy Tarleton's arm with the other. "We live on Queen's Park Road, number one-twenty-one Queen's Park Road."

Nancy Tarleton nodded and said, "Well my goodness, you could just knock me over with a feather. Now, let me think, one-twenty-one, one-twenty-one, oh that's the nice end down there, isn't it Larry?"

The Indiana Jones hat nodded in agreement.

"There are some gorgeous houses down there, and the country club and all."

Mary Helen Hager smiled magnanimously.

Then, after taking a second to realise that she had accidentally, in her excitement, entangled Anne

Boleyn in her necklace, said, "Yes, we like to think so, but we don't see it as different from any place else. For us, folks are folks, wherever they are, and one-twenty-one, well, that's just home to us. You see, I was born and raised in the area."

At this, she closed her eyes to emphasise her obvious modesty.

She was only interrupted in her reverie by a tug on her sleeve. She spun round to see Margaret Burke Ragsdale and husband Scoot Ragsdale standing behind her.

"You went galloping off and left me," Margaret Burke Ragsdale said.

Her quilted handbag was a shade darker than Mary Helen Hager's. Scoot's hat had a little bit deeper crease in the crown than Wendell's.

"I did no such thing," Mary Helen Hager protested, knowing full well that she had done exactly that, "And anyway, I want you to meet some people I have just met. Nancy and Larry, this is my oldest friend Margaret Burke Ragsdale and her husband Scoot. These are the Tarletons."

The couples shook hands.

"Oh look, you found the Christmas ornaments," Margaret Burke Ragsdale said, finally spotting the showcase.

"Yes, but forget about that for the moment. You are never going to believe it, but guess where Nancy and Larry are from."

Margaret Burke Ragsdale turned back to the couple and gave them a good look over, perhaps believing that studying them would somehow reveal their origins.

"Guess," Mary Helen Hager demanded.

"I don't know, where?"

The Tarletons stood there, beaming, pleased to be a part of the business.

"They are from Middlesboro," Mary Helen Hager shouted.

Margaret Burke Ragsdale put on an expression of utter shock, not able to imagine that anyone else in Middlesboro would ever have happened upon the idea of travelling to Britain.

"Really?" she said.

"And that's not all," Mary Helen Hager continued. "Get this: they live on Queen's Park Road. Can you believe it?"

Margaret Burke Ragsdale managed to ratchet up her look of surprise another notch.

"Are you pulling my leg? And y'all met just now?"

"Just now, right here in front of the these gorgeous little Christmas ornaments," Mary Helen Hager said.

She was feeling quite pleased with herself, having discovered these nice people from back home, and she was very happy that Margaret Burke Ragsdale had found her here, not only allowing her the means of revelling in the sheer spectacle of this chance encounter, but also providing her with a witness who could verify it all once they were back home. It was going to make the best story to tell back in Middlesboro. She would have to invite the Tarletons over for cocktails, she mused. She could see herself standing in the sun room at home, with its wicker and floral prints, regaling all the neighbours about how they had met at Windsor Castle of all places.

While Margaret Burke Ragsdale exchanged pleasantries with the new acquaintances, asking when they had arrived and such, it suddenly occurred to Mary Helen Hager how odd it was that seeing as how they were not only from the same town but also lived on the same road, that she didn't already know the Tarletons. Now Queen's Park Road, it was true, was a long road, and it even stretched over across town into some new, not as nice neighbourhoods, but it did seem inconceivable that she would not have run into the Tarletons before.

Her curiosity piqued, she asked, "Now what number Queen's Park Road do y'all live at Nancy?"

She was dying to ascertain how they lived on the same road and yet not managed to meet. She was sure that they would all have a great laugh over the sheer inconceivable, accidental folly of it.

"Oh, we live at twelve-eighty-six Queen's Park Road, further up than y'all do," Nancy Tarleton said, "not too far from the Piggly Wiggly."

She carried on for a bit, chattering on in the same vein, but Mary Helen Hager did not hear her. She had ceased to take in anything after "twelve-eighty-six," having been struck, somewhere behind the eye sockets, with what could only be described as a shock, something akin to a bolt of electricity. The smile on her face became decidedly fixed and her eyes took on a rather puzzled look. She wondered for a second if perhaps she could have accidentally brushed Anne Boleyn up against a live wire somewhere.

When Nancy Tarleton finished speaking, Mary Helen Hager stood there silent. Then, suddenly realising where she was, and looking a little flustered, she uttered, "Oh."

You could just make out the colour slowly fading from her frosted lips. She suddenly felt flushed and hot inside her rain jacket.

"Yes, we live further up than y'all do, and its not nearly as nice as down your way," Nancy Tarleton rattled on, "But we love it over there. It is so convenient to the mall and all, except for the train, but we do keep hoping that one day they'll do something about those train tracks. Lord, sometimes you're waiting for fifteen minutes for the train to pass through on the its way over to the steam plant. Anyway though, it must be something else to have the park right on your doorstep like y'all do. And the Azalea Festival, I nearly forgot about that. We drive around looking at all the beautiful yards every year. Are y'all involved with that?"

Like an over-leavened cake in the oven, Mary Helen Hager's face fell. Her hand dropped from Nancy Tarleton's arm as though it were weighted down by some heavy piece of metal. She attempted a rather sickly smile. The effervescence that had practically overcome her a few moments earlier was nowhere to be found, having been dampened by the cold splash of the Tarleton's address.

"We sure are," she said, taking a step backward, dropping Anne Boleyn in the process, and crushing her under the sole of a walking shoe.

"I wish we had some of those nice azaleas on our side of town. Seems like all we get are Dollar Generals. Anyhow, here we are, neighbours, at Windsor Castle, where the Queen of England lives," said Nancy Tarleton, "Traveling halfway around the world only to run into good old folks from just down the road, I can hardly believe it."

She reached out to take Mary Helen Hager's hand but found only an empty void where it had been just a moment before.

"Uh huh," said Mary Helen Hager, taking another step backward and staring down at a flattened Anne Boleyn on the floor.

"Are y'all here with anybody else?" Margaret Burke Ragsdale asked, not aware of Mary Helen Hager's growing discomfiture.

"We're here with two other couples from our church, Westside Baptist," Nancy Tarleton said, "But they're not with us today. We had the option on our tour of going to Windsor Castle or Legoland, and they went to Legoland."

Mary Helen Hager fumbled with her raincoat for moment. Then all of a sudden, feigning a surprised look at her watch, she said in mock astonishment, "Lord look at the time. Wendell, quit dragging your feet. We've got to go. We've got that church to see down at the bottom of the hill before we're done. Y'all are going to have to excuse us."

She directed a cursive look at the Tarletons

and worked up a smile, saying, "I can't tell you how nice it was meeting you both. Now listen here, y'all have a nice vacation, alright? Bye now."

At this she turned and bolted straight for the door, leaving Nancy and Larry Tarleton and the Ragsdales standing there. Nancy Tarleton, pressing her outstretched thumb and forefinger into her own neck, as if she were only about to discover in the next few minutes that it had been sliced right through, kept a broad if somewhat odd smile on her face.

Margaret Burke Ragsdale, never the quickest one, called after Mary Helen Hager, "Where are you running off to now?"

Wendell smiled and said as he turned to leave, "Well, I reckon she's ready to go. Y'all take care. Maybe we'll see you back home."

Larry Tarleton and Scoot Ragsdale both grinned and tapped their index fingers on the brim of their hats in response.

Mary Helen Hager was nearly halfway down the hill before Wendell caught up with her, her walking shoes pumping rhythmically and the tails of her green raincoat flapping behind her.

"I thought you were hell-bent on buying some of them Christmas decorations," he said.

"No, I don't want any of those old things. Once I got a good look at them, I though they looked tacky. Probably made in China anyway," she said.

They walked in silence for a moment, the Gothic pinnacles of St. George's Chapel looming overhead.

"And you sure couldn't get yourself out of that gift shop fast enough," he said.

/ "Well I'm sorry as I can be," she said looking straight ahead, "but I didn't come all the way to England to hobnob with the likes of them that live up on the trashy end of Queen's Park Road. I could do that at home."

"Well all right then, but you are the one who was making over them and was introducing them to everybody, and they *are* neighbours."

"What are you talking about? People who live way over yonder in the twelve hundred block are hardly neighbours, for goodness sake," she said, trying to hide her irritation. "Now don't get me wrong, she was just as sweet as she could be, bless her heart; what was her name, Naomi?/But you know good and well that we don't have anything to do with anybody from way across town. What on earth could we possibly talk to them about? Lord, they're not even in the same school zone. I mean for goodness sake, I certainly can't be expected to stand around gabbing with a bunch of people we have not one thing in common with. Now let's go see this church that we've paid good money to see, this King George's Chapel or whatever it is."

She looked straight ahead and set her shoulders in a manner that said that was the end of the matter. After a minute, she turned her attention to the huge pile of the Chapel in front of her.

"So what's in here?" she asked, having successfully changed the subject.

"Henry the Eighth," said Wendell, studying his pamphlet.

"Henry the Eighth? The one who cut all his wives' heads off? Oh lord," she said..

"Says here that his first wife was a foreign one, and he divorced her. His second wife was an English one, and he had her head chopped off."

"Well, I guess they weren't as advanced as nowadays," she mused.

Yes, Mary Helen Hager knew what was what, and this was turning out, to all appearances, to be one of those moments when she could congratulate herself on knowing just what was what. She decided right then and there to put out of her mind forever, the image of a Christmas tree, loaded down with colourful, hand-embroidered ornaments, standing in the living room of twelve-eighty-six Queen's Park Road. Although she may not have been able to put her finger on it, she knew all too well that there are none so far as those who are near. From her vantage point of several thousand miles' distance, it was indisputable that that was simply an address ten blocks too far, and yet at the very same time, an address ten blocks - indeed a world - too near.

Running Smack into General Sherman

I

"They've run into something. It's not going," Colin said.

"The hell it's not," Will spat back.

The two brothers, alarmed by his outburst, interpreted it as a cue to double down on their efforts.

"Move it this way, Andy," the one huffed to the other.

"I 'ave, Tony," the other answered in protest.

"Take it over this way, Andy," the one said.

"I 'ave, Tony," the other one answered.

They strained, grunting and sweating, attempting to push, pull, or scrape the great bulk of it past the confined turning of the stairwell, a space echoey and oppressive as a cave. The more they struggled, however, the less it seemed to move, as if either it were growing or the stairwell were slowly contracting around it.

How has it come to this? Will pondered. Standing there in the close damp of the stairwell, he

191

asked himself, *How can this even be happening?* They all stood there, the four of them, Will, Colin, and the two brothers. Sweat was dripping off of the fraternal brows of the two furniture removers, who looking bewildered, were awaiting something, some direction, some intervention, anything. Will bit his lip, wrung his hands for the thousandth time, and said nothing. The panic that was welling up inside of him could erupt and spill over, were he not careful.

"I don't fink we're going to get it up there, mate," one of them, red-faced, finally offered down in Will's direction.

"In fact," he said, "I fink it's stuck."

Will received this last bit as if someone had punched him in the gut. There on the wall he could make out the evidence of an excruciating streak of deep red. He turned around and walked down the steps, kicking an empty syringe out of his path. He intended to sit down on the bottom step, but seeing the tell-tale bloom of dried piss on it stopped him.

How has it come to this? he repeated to himself again, momentarily bowing his head and resting it in his cupped hands. Then he noticed the smell. It had crept into his nostrils, like a thief in the night, but he hadn't caught wind of it, until now. That smell, that unmistakable smell – dust, cheap cleanser, and old piss, the hallmark of every stair-well in every Council estate in London - was assaulting his nostrils. That he was familiar with the permeating stink of it, that he was experiencing it, caused a wave of disgust and shame to sweep over him. Funny how they all smell exactly the same. Just as London's streets have a particular odour, a mixture of chip fat and drains, so do all the Council estates.

He suppressed a shudder of repulsion. *I was not meant for this*, he thought to himself. On the dusty concrete in front of him lay an empty crisp packet, gaudy and cheap-looking in the blue, fluorescent gloom. He shook his head dismally. *They all eat crisps*, he thought, *and they always, always throw the empty packet on the floor*. The admission of this was proof positive of the pathetic level of existence he was being forced to endure. The crisp packet was practically mocking him from the floor; and the trashy, pale children, with their cheap track-suit bottoms and foul mouths, who had no doubt thrown that packet down, although they were nowhere to be found at present, were mocking him as well.

"What are we going to do, mate?" one of the brothers called down.

He couldn't really tell them apart, these brothers. They were, to be honest, identical to him, a blur of London working-class patter, both with faces like an unfinished police sketch. They were neighbours from the old estate, ostensibly furniture removers, but really just two work-shy "geezers," who still lived with their mother and happened to own a removals van.

"I sure as shit don't know," Will said.

This he addressed in the direction of the open door in front of him. He wrung his hands again, blew the breath sharply out of his mouth, and turned, taking in the entire ridiculous scene anew: the stairwell with its pointless, brutalist turnings and angles, the rubbish, the piss, the smell, Colin standing there, useless as usual, and the two movers in their obligatory white trainers, sweating; and in the centre of it all, wedged-in at an ungainly angle, a large piece of furniture, a large, old, cupboard to be exact. The incongruity of it all could not be lost on anyone. The contrast of the dark, smooth, piece of antique furniture, something obviously, from its appearance, well-looked after and cared for, in this forlorn, dank, and best-forgotten spot would have been comic had it not been so pitiful.

II

Will had been in London for nearly six years, having moved from New York to live with his partner Colin. Originally from North Carolina, he had migrated to New York after grad school, like so many Southerners before him. It was there that he had met Colin, who was visiting on holiday. Within nine months of their meeting, Colin had invited him to move to London. Refusing to overly deliberate on the idea, Will accepted the invitation on what could only be called a whim. This was an impulsive, even cavalier move on his part, which he, Will, freely acknowledged, and yet did not allow to sway his decision.

"You ain't getting any younger," he told himself in some sort of attempt at justification for moving halfway around the world, and at that he had packed all that he could fit into a suitcase and shipped a couple of boxes over to London, the remainder of the contents of his apartment being left in the hands of an acquaintance who was serving as boarder.

He had moved into Colin's small, one-bedroom flat, which Will had immediately realised, was uncomfortably cramped with the two of them. However, as Will was not immediately able to work in the UK - and Colin never did work it seemed - the prospect of moving was a distant one, at least for the present. It was only after a few years, when Will had finally been reunited with all of his belongings, that the two of them came up with the idea of putting Colin's name on the waiting list for a Council flat. If they waited long enough, they could obtain a larger place, and eventually, Will learned much to own surprise, purchase it as well. It took three years of slowly climbing the waiting list, but finally, one day word came from the local Council that they would be offered a flat.

Will had imagined a quirky, older, if some-what faded, Victorian property on a tree-lined street, something not unlike the string of eccentric, cheap but somehow charming, apartments that he had inhabited over the years in the US. What they were offered was quite a different story, dramatically different to what he had imagined or even could fathom. It was only ten minutes' walk, and yet it was a world away. When they reached the bleak, windswept estate where the Council official met them at the foot of the looming tower block and ushered them into the creaky lift, redolent with the stench of urine, Will began to feel the unease within himself rising, rising as though it were in tandem with the lift itself. Once on the fifth floor landing, which was littered with old - and they were later to learn stolen - bicycle parts, she unlocked the door to the flat. As the door opened, they were practically knocked backward by the overpowering odour of musty carpet and old cigarettes. "Jesus!" Will uttered, in spite of himself. The walls, all peeling woodchip wallpaper, had at one time been painted, depending on the room, lurid pink, lurid purple, or lurid turquoise, all of which was now patinated with the uniform, yellow film of years of nicotine.

The woman from the Council chirped, "All it needs is a lick of paint."

Will, shaking his head in disgust, after five minutes walked out, grumbling, "No way. No frigging way."

Colin stayed behind and told the Council woman that they would take the flat, signing the papers right then and there, and that was that. Six weeks later, after spending hundreds of pounds having the walls replastered and painted, the exposed wiring hidden, and some timber flooring installed, they had made the place just habitable enough to move into.

III

The two brothers continued to stare down at

Will from their position on either side of the cupboard, above him in the winding stairwell.

"What should we do, mate?" the one repeated.

At first it had appeared that the bulky piece of furniture was going be moved up the stairwell without too much problem, successfully missing obstacles of the maze of balustrades and claustrophobic, concrete walls and ceilings, but once they got to the second floor, the staircase inextricably changed its course, and the cupboard, manhandled by the movers, ran right into a niggardly, obtuse triangulation of concrete, getting itself stuck in the process.

"Well, we certainly can't leave it here, can we? Do you think you can at least get it back down the stairs?" Will asked, his voice no longer able to mask how close he was to crying.

"Yeah, we'll shift it mate." one of them reassured him.

They weren't that bright, but they could at least recognise that he was upset. At that, the one turned to confer with his brother.

"Right Andy, now if I pull this way, you lift over there, right mate?"

Will walked outside and left them to it, unable to witness any more. He was at the end of his rope. Outside, beside himself with nerves, he paced around the area adjacent to the stairwell entrance. There were some gates to an underground parking garage to his left and the back of the local shop, a lowbrow supermarket chain, to his right, each one more desolate than the other. He was certain that the noise, the tortured screaking of trapped corners, like something being confined in a vault, could be heard all the way down the street.

Above him, casting a gloomy shadow over it all, loomed the depressing tower block, a grimy, concrete monolith draped in filthy green netting, a latticework ostensibly to keep the pigeons from roosting on the balconies, but in actuality a device to catch the incessant array of rubbish thrown out by the occupants. A mere glance at the bulging contents trapped in the bottom of it at the first floor level seemed to confirm the situation. In it hung, like forgotten, rotting sea creatures caught in some bizarre fishing expedition, were miscellaneous articles of clothing, take away containers, rags, empty beer tins, and soiled nappies. Behind him issued the noise from the within the stairwell, the animated screeching, the hollow bumping, and the shouts of the brothers. He shook his head dismally. Within a few minutes, however, the noise transformed itself, the echoing diminishing until he could clearly hear the laboured huffing and grunting of the brothers approaching just behind him. As he turned, he was confronted with the full profile of the cupboard standing there before him, liberated from the confines of the sepulchral stairwell.

IV

This old piece of furniture before him could not have been any more unsuited for life in London, made as it was for living conditions in nineteenth-century North Carolina, a balmy region on the American southeast coast, an area of the country where dwellings were typified by large rooms, generous spaces, and high ceilings. London, with its tiny flats and awkward staircases made for a cramped existence for such an artefact from a more commodious age and locale. In its dimensions, the cupboard stood about seven foot tall and four wide. Stylistically, it was what old fashioned antique dealers would call a "country piece," by which they would hope to invoke in it a certain quaint and naïve quality, all redolent of folksy ways and upright values. Whether this was inherent in the cupboard or not, Will knew it to possess so many of the desirable traits of country furniture: it was playful in its detailing; it was full of character and completely unique; it was utterly charming in its folk interpretation of a more academic style; and perhaps most vitally, it intimately illuminated the artistic expression of its maker, the maker in this instance being Will's great-grandfather James Crowell.

In colour, it was a rich, dark red-brown, personifying a certain vitality and vigour, Will liked to imagine, being made from Southern Yellow Pine, or "heart pine" as Southern folk are fond of saying. Four panelled and moulded doors, two larger ones above, two smaller below, were the principal elements of the façade. In true country fashion, these doors were kept closed by means of a charming, hand-carved propeller-shaped piece of wood that acted as a latch. Playfully spinning this novel little device, which was secured to the front middle rail so that it could catch all four doors, had been the idle pastime of countless generations of children over the years, Will included.

The lower end of the cupboard was treated in a manner that could only be described as whimsical. A deep scalloped skirt finished off the bottom of the carcass, something that reminded Will of the fanciful calligraphy seen on antique Fraktur from early North Carolina. And the considerable bulk of the piece was thrown into high relief by the way it diminished and eventually terminated onto four, almost impossibly small, feet. In contrast to the lower portion, however, the top was made up simply of a very wide, overhanging board stretched across the upper part of the carcass. It always, to Will's way of thinking, looked a bit incomplete, and close scrutiny had revealed nail holes that indicated that there was once, sometime in the past, a more fitting top piece or crown. This, in the course of the years, had probably been sacrificed when some poor soul had been confronted with a low ceiling or a tight staircase, a grim fact certainly not lost on Will today.

However, of all the architectural elements of the cupboard, Will's favourites were the sides of it. Replicating the doors on the front, they were panelled and moulded, which didn't really seem to be necessary for a piece of cabinetry no deeper than it was. It could have been easily constructed with plain, wide planks, and yet it was not. His great-grandfather had demonstrably gone to more trouble than was needed, and the fact that this feature had been time-consuming to make and not even necessary in a purely utilitarian, construction sense, is what delighted Will no end. These side panels embodied a kind of generous elegance, an overabundance, which elevated the cupboard beyond the ordinary. They came to be, in Will's mind, a sort of visual symbol for his great-grandfather's family in general. His people weren't the common run, but something a cut above, just as this piece of old furniture so elegantly demon-strated.

V

Out of doors, dwarfed by the sooty tower blocks, and standing here on the cracked, grease-stained concrete of the estate, the cupboard did not look nearly as large as it had done in the cramped stairwell. That said, it still towered over him. Will tried not to notice the newly acquired, ugly abrasions at the corners.

"Now mate, what should we do?" one of the brothers asked.

"Oh god, I don't know. I really don't know." Will said shaking his head.

"Is it really valuable?" the other brother asked.

"Well no," he said, trying to hide his irritation at what he thought was a rather pointless question. "But I did ship it all the way over here from North Carolina. It's from the family."

"His grandfather made it," Colin piped up.

"Great-grandfather," Will corrected.

"Shit, it must be really old then," one of the brothers added.

"Old enough I suppose…old enough to know better," Will said, wearying of the conversation.

"And I guess selling it is out of the question, eh mate?" the other brother asked.

Will knew that the brothers often sold the odd piece of furniture, anything that they came across in their removal work, to the junk shop on North End Road.

"Yes, out of the question." he said, closing his eyes in exhaustion.

It looked so out of place here: the crassness of the surroundings were an affront to the sheer dignity of its features and the chasteness of its construction. There was a convulsion in Will's throat, and he struggled to fight back a choking wail. He felt that all of what this piece of furniture embodied, all that it symbolised was being bruised, sullied, and molested. It were as though he were dragging his great-grandparents themselves, and the rest of his family for that matter, through the reeking, unwholesome, stairwell, through the crisp packets and pigeon droppings.

"Why don't we put it back on the van, mate?" one of the brothers offered. "Tony and I don't have any jobs for a couple of days. It can stay on there until you figure out what to do."

For once, Will was actually touched by them. "Are you sure?" he asked. "That would be great if we could."

"No problems mate," the other one said.

Within a few minutes, they had it hoisted back up into the van. Everything else from the old flat had been moved the day before. They had left the cupboard for last, having already realised that it would not fit into the smelly, stuttering lift with its low ceiling.

"When you figure out what to do, just come over and knock on me Mum's door, mate," one of them said to him from the open window in the cab of the van. And with that, they drove off, leaving him and Colin standing there, alone save for a few smutty pigeons that were lazily pecking at some old cigarette butts.

As they stood there, wondering what next to do, a pear-shaped teenage girl came round the corner from the shop, waddling behind a cheap push chair that was loaded down with several bulging carrier bags hanging off of the handles. Seated in the chair was an angry-looking toddler, bullying a dummy in its mouth. The girl, Will thought, looked like so many of them around here: a sullen, vacant expression on her face, her hair scraped up tight into a "scrunchy," and gold hoops the size of salad plates hanging from her ears. Behind her toddled a plump, ginger child, no more than three or four years old, with pierced ears. The mother lumbered by, not acknowledging either Will or Colin there in front of her. The child, however, stopped and blinked up enquiringly at them.

"Hello," Will said to her.

Her mother walked on a few steps before she

turned around, her face like a tin of Spam, and shouted, "Chantelle, come on. I mean it, you little cunt."

The child dropped its head and walked silently on. Colin looked over at Will with raised eyebrows, placing a hand on his hip.

Nothing surprised Will anymore. Whereas at one time, he would have been aghast at a mother talking to her child in that fashion, the few short weeks of his introduction to this estate had inculcated him for such. Mothers, children, all of them, he had come to learn, could have mouths like gutters, and short fuses to boot. However, he could not dwell on that today; he had his own, more urgent matters to attend to, and he was immediately drawn back to the fiasco of what had just transpired. He could not get his cupboard up to the new flat, either by the lift, or as he had just had the traumatic experience of witnessing, up the stairs. He was at a loss of what to do, and this was fuelling his growing sense of panic.

This was not simply some ordinary piece of furniture, or even a much-loved antique. This was a piece of family history that he had known all of his life, an object lovingly and painstakingly crafted by his great-grandfather over one hundred and twenty years previously. This was something, like a companion, that had been with him throughout his sojourns in North Carolina, New York, and London. Of all his complicated and sometimes even tortured relationship with his family history, his ancestry, this artefact, this hulking piece of pine wood was the most potent symbol of all that his inherited past stood for, all that it meant. He feared that he, as the inheritor, the curator of his past, was just on the precipice of failing miserably in this, his appointed role.

And now the cupboard was standing forlornly in the back of a removals van, with no known way to move it into his flat. What was he to do? Something that had been in his family, indeed had been created by his family, was not something that one day, you simply shrugged your shoulders at and said, "Oh well, can't get it up the stairs. Hey ho." He visibly shuddered, then caught himself and turned with Colin to go upstairs, upstairs to what was going to be their new home. Whether it was going to be the new home for his family heirloom remained to be seen.

VI

The early details of the cupboard, this venerated piece of his family history, like that of so many relics, while tolerably shrouded in mystery, had a familiar, decreed story nonetheless, one that Will had eagerly learned from his earliest days. Family tradition maintained that Will's great-grandfather, James Ardrey Crowell, had constructed it. It was said that James, himself a seventh-generation descendent of those hearty, fearless Germans and Scots-Irish who had settled Piedmont North Carolina the century before, had fashioned it after his marriage in 1883 for his bride, a young woman named Mary Jane Mullis. He and Mary Jane lived happily for some years in Mecklenburg County, and she bore him three daughters, before she suddenly contracted and succumbed to "the Consumption." With Mary Jane dead, James found himself not even twenty-five years of age, a widower, with three young daughters to raise. This was a low ebb for the family, but fortunately, James soon met a red-haired school teacher named Frances Stinson, whom he married and with whom he started a family, the youngest child of their five being Will's grandmother.

The cupboard was incorporated into the new household, as were James's three daughters, who were adopted by the pious, God-fearing Frances. The girls regarded her as their Mama, as she became, with the passage of time, the only mother that they could remember. Still, it was never forgotten for whom the cupboard was originally intended, and the piece of cabinetry came to be seen not simply as a piece of furniture, but as a love token for a spouse and mother that cruel death had stolen away. Thus, from the very outset, it had been infused with an effluvium of solemnity, something that permeated it and remained a fixture of it throughout the years. It was no mere piece of furniture. It remained a well-loved object in the household for many years, even after James's death.

This situation only changed late in the 1920's, when Frances, now a widow and with the last of her children - Will's grandmother to be exact - married off, she decided to "break up housekeeping" for good. She went to living a peripatetic existence, moving between the homes of her children, and as she no longer had a household of her own, the family furniture was dispersed, including the cupboard. That it was originally made for James's first wife Mary Jane, offers somewhat of an explanation of the cupboard's subsequent history, for it was decided that it would go to one of her children, one of the three girls, Frances's step-daughters.

These three were improbably named, Bess, Eck, and Odd, a colourful set of names that was never lost on the ever impressionable Will. With Bess, the eldest, having died in childbirth as a young woman, it fell to the next in line, the exotically named Eck to look after the cupboard. It was she who daubed it in thick crème enamel, and it was she who applied colourful stencils: cascading flowers set within neo-classical roundels, to each of the lower doors. It was said that she always kept caged canaries. The household conjures a picture of a pretty, pleasant domesticity, full of shades of sunny yellow, stylised flowers, curtains, and singing birds. These were the glowing, and in Will's mind, slightly chimerical surroundings of this old piece of furniture in those days.

It was only after the death of the enchanted Aunt Eck that the cupboard came back into the possession of his great-grandmother Frances, now in her eighties, and it is here that Will, as a small child in his grandparents' house, first encountered it. By that time, considered hopelessly old-fashioned, it was painted sanitary white and stood in a niche in the "breakfast nook," just off the kitchen, of the rambling, comfortable, old family home.

Sometimes Will would stand before the cupboard and spin the little door-keep round and round (which was just at his eye-level) until someone, usually his grandmother, who was excitable, would say to him, "Stop that racket, Sonny." Other times, he would pivot the doors fully open, pulling them back against the jambs of the niche. This would create a tiny, enclosed space, just large enough for a boy to hide in. Here he would place himself, listening in his dark, snug cell, to the adults at the supper table opposite going about their business. The topics were familiar to his ears: his grandfather launching into a comic tirade about the shortcomings of the negroes, and his grandmother shrilly warning her Mama, his great-grandmother Frances, about her nonagenarian table habits. "Land sakes Mama," she would scold, "Can you not see how much pepper you're shaking on that?"

As the years progressed, and his grandfather died, soon followed by his beloved great-grandmother, Will's grandmother found herself in a "changing" neighbourhood, all alone in a large house, which seemed to require constant upkeep. The raking up of the leaves alone, dropped from the countless, tall, oak trees that covered the property, took weeks to accomplish. With some deliberation, it was decided that she should move into smaller quarters.

Will was a teenager by this time, and one day while they were seated at the kitchen table eating a piece of strawberry custard pie, his grandmother shocked him by asking, "Sonny, do you reckon that you would want to have Papa's cupboard?"

He put down his fork, not knowing what to say. He had always hoped that the cupboard might one day be his and for years had made no bones about the fact that he had wanted it, but he did not know if he would actually ever be given it or not. While no one else in the family had expressed any interest in it whatsoever - large, cumbersome pieces of nineteenth-century furniture were not what most people envisaged in their modern, ranch-style houses in the 1970's - his grandmother had a propensity for giving family heirlooms away to her favourite brother's children who lived down in Florida. That is how his great-grandmother's spinning wheel had disappeared. One day it was there, in its place in a corner of the front room, then the next thing he knew, it had been shipped off to Jacksonville, because a second cousin of his had once remarked on how much she liked it.

So, given recent history, he did not count on having anything from his ancestors until he actually had it. Looking up from his pie, he spluttered across the table that yes, he would very much like to have the cupboard. Within a few weeks, he, his father, and his father's buddy from work, Joe, had humped it out of his grandmother's house and into his own allotted half of the outhouse that his father used for storage and Will used for his "antiques" that he had been collecting since he was a child. There were old bottles of all types and sizes, cowbells and other farm implements gleaned from his grandfather's barn, and even an old wood-burning range that had once stood proudly in his grandmother's kitchen. And now this was to be the new home of the cupboard.

"Boy, where do you want it?" his father huffed as he and Joe struggled to manoeuvre the sheer weight of it through the door of the outhouse.

Will had cleared a spot for it, the choicest position in the entire shed, and it was to this spot that he nervously directed the two sweating men.

He had been stripping furniture for about five years, and had become quaint adept at it, having the patience and temperament needed to meticulously lift the paint without damaging the easily scarred wood underneath. Practically no sooner had the cupboard taken its place in his shed, than he got out his gloves, scrapers, and gallon tin of paint stripper. His grandmother, several years earlier, had painted it an avocado green and had over-coated this with a murky, sepia-toned wash. This, at the time, was called "antiquing," which confused Will no end, as he had never in all his life seen an actual, authentic antique painted anything resembling this. He carefully poured some of the thick, noxious liquid into an empty peanut butter jar, and taking an old paint brush, he neatly daubed it onto the front of the cupboard in a neat square. Within a few minutes, the dull green of the antique finish was wrinkled and checked. Using his scraper, he gently lifted the green to reveal white underneath, the pure white that he remembered from his childhood.

He quickly anointed the spot with more stripper and waited for it to act. Soon, the white crazed in the same fashion as the green had done, and he lifted it off. This revealed another white layer, for which he repeated the process yet again. He went through white strata; then through several yellow ones, from the era of Aunt Eck he surmised. He was amazed at the thickness of the paint, all the numerous laminations. As he was removing it, exhuming layer after layer, he had reached that sort of tranquil, meditative state, which he had come to recognise as a part of the methodical stripping process. Without needing to direct himself, he lathered the stripper on yet another coat of yellow paint and let it stand. He noticed something was transpiring: the odour. He knew from experience that the smell of the stripper changes, becoming almost woody-fragrant, when you have finally reached the wood and were just before revealing it. It was a scent that Will had learned to detect and to rejoice in. He took his scraper and ever so gingerly lifted the papery yellow coating from the wood, suddenly exposing the pine, pine which had not seen the light of day in nearly a century.

"Wow, oh my lord," he exclaimed to himself in astonishment.

He hadn't expected what was suddenly revealed. The old wood was a rich, dark reddish-brown; it appeared that it had originally been tinted and sealed with a deep, ruddy finish, something more akin to the treatment of expensive cabinet wood, not homely old pine, which was more times than not simply and cheaply painted. He carefully cleaned the square with stripper and old rag, then stood back to examine his handiwork. The small window of the square revealed a timber with a close, even grain, the hallmark of old heart pine, and the finish pointed to an aesthetic process that had obviously been present in the workings of his great-grandfather. By staining and finishing it in such a manner, he was obviously intending to raise this piece of furniture from the mere mundane, from being simply a utilitarian kitchen store cupboard, to something finer. Will was thrilled, although somewhat daunted at the realisation of how thick the paint was and how much work would be required to remove it.

As he stood there basking in the wonderful aroma of newly stripped antique wood, he realised that his grandmother was coming for supper later. She will be interested in this, he thought to himself, and she will appreciate the fineness of this finish revealed, something, after all, that her own father had orchestrated. He anxiously awaited her arrival that afternoon, meeting her at her old blue Chevrolet as she parked at the far corner of the drive and insisted that she follow him out to the outhouse before she went inside the house.

"I've got something to show you." Will told her.

"What is it Sonny?" she protested, not wanting to turn the heel of her Spectator pumps in the soft ground.

"You'll see," he said, directing her into the shed.

Once she had stepped over the threshold, he said, "Look," while he pointed to the stripped square on the cupboard.

His grandmother stood there for a moment saying nothing, her black handbag hanging from her right hand.

"Great day in the morning, Sonny, what have you done?" she asked in astonishment.

"I've stripped some of that old paint off it," he said, suddenly feeling a bit unsure of the situation.

"Why you've ruined it, Sonny," she shouted in exasperation. "Why would you want to do that?"

At that she and her handbag left the shed.

Of course, even with his grandmother's disapproval, he carried on, little by little, stripping away the old paint, revealing more and more of the rich brown pine. The red stain, what he had surmised to be the original finish, was unlike anything he had encountered before. He had no idea what his great-grandfather had utilised, but whatever it was, it was strong stuff. The wood was permanently coloured, and if any touched his bare skin, it dyed it red, leaving an almost indelible tinge. Diligently retaining as much of the ruddy-brown colour as possible, Will eventually removed all of the later accretions. He worked over his school breaks and on the weekends until he had pored over the entire piece. After several years, he could finally announce that the refinishing process was at last complete. The finished product was truly lovely to behold, looking even nicer than Will had ever imagined. Even his grandmother came to accept the new look, utilising the aegis of old age to conveniently forget her earlier crankiness. In fact, over time, she came to believe that it was she who was responsible for it being transformed into the beautiful condition that it was now in. Will, having been brought up to never contradict the elderly, said nothing; he was happy enough.

After he graduated from university and left his parents' house, the cupboard followed him. Wherever he happened to be living in North Carolina, which usually seemed to be some variation of old, rundown, pre-war apartment, it always made up a part of his decor. Even if the heating was sporadic and the paint peeling in these places, at least the rooms were spacious and the ceilings high, just perfect for his beloved piece of furniture. Later on, when he decided to move to New York, things proved a bit more problematic. For ten hours, without stopping, he had driven a rented furniture van, its sole contents being the cupboard, up from North Carolina. He had crossed over the George Washington Bridge in the dark of the evening, only later learning, much to his horror, that moving vans were not allowed on the bridge and he had broken the law. It was late at night when he finally reached Thompson Street down in Greenwich Village where he was living. An old friend from North Carolina, who like himself now called New York home, met him there and they struggled, straining and panting to the point of complete exhaustion, to hump the cupboard up the three flights of the old tenement building into his tiny, albeit expensive, two room apartment. It was a cramped little place which overlooked the back of a pizzeria and smelled like the Chinese restaurant next door. It had high ceilings, however, which suited the proportions of the cupboard. Oddly, although far from North Carolina, it seemed strangely at home in the city, and the storage it provided was a boon in such tight quarters.

A few year later, however, he had met Colin and was on the move once again, this time to London. He had paid a company in New York to collect his furniture and other belongings in the Thompson Street apartment and ship them abroad. The shippers collected the cupboard from Greenwich Village and had taken it up to the Bronx, where it was loaded onto a container ship bound for Ireland. He would never forget his utter surprise at receiving that telephone call on Christmas morning from the two Irishmen. They had loaded his belongings onto a lorry in Dublin, had taken the ferry to Liverpool, had driven all night, and were now in London wishing to make delivery. The cupboard arrived at the London flat completely wrapped in brown paper like a giant gift, on Christmas afternoon, just as the Queen's speech was being broadcast on the BBC. He tore through the paper like a child, revealing the familiar, deep, reddish-brown wood. Throwing open the doors and casting his eyes upon the reassuring red interior, he stuck his head inside and took a deep whiff. The scent was still there, that particular odour of old oil cloth mingled with a redolence of ancient country ham from days gone by.

VII

Will and Colin stepped out of the lift onto the landing with its clutter of mysterious bicycle parts. The piss-heavy smell from the lift was replaced with the one of old concrete impregnated with dust and filth. They had not actually met the neighbours on the far side of the landing yet, but from the looks of the front door and surrounding area, Will had a pretty good inkling of what sort they were going to prove to be. He quickly opened the door to the flat where he was confronted with cardboard boxes stacked to the ceiling. At the least, the persistent, clean odour of new paint offered some relief to his nostrils. Colin went straight to the spare room where the computer was awaiting him to play some sort of game. He had unpacked just enough to set up the computer, desk and chair, and now considered himself finished. All the rest would be for Will to sort out, as usual. A flicker of rage came upon him, but he stifled it. If he lost his temper at his partner's idleness, Colin would only pout for the rest of the day. Saying anything went nowhere.

"Don't you think we should unpack some of these boxes?" Will shouted toward the bedroom where Colin was already sitting in front of the screen, engrossed in supplying troops or something to some imaginary village.

"What?" was Colin's reply.

"I said, don't you think we should unpack some of these boxes?" he repeated more loudly, only half-attempting to hide his growing irritation

. There was no reply; so Will set about inspecting the numerous brown cardboard cartons. As he stood there in the odd, polygon-shaped foyer, he took note of the spot where he had planned to place the cupboard. He shook his head miserably and determined to make himself busy. He reached up for a box, lifted it down to the floor and opened up the flaps. He pulled out some towels and laid them on the floor. Below them was an old-fashioned, black-painted, tin box, elegantly striped in gold and red lining. This he lifted out and placed on the floor as well. He opened it up to reveal a stack of old photographs. He knew them all by heart, without even having to pull them out to look at them, and he was fully aware that there were photographs in the box that portrayed his great-grandfather James, and his progress through the years. He could well remember that in decades past, whenever they were brought out, first his great-grandmother, then later by his grandmother, there was a certain air of solemnity that surrounded their exposition and even a degree of formal ceremony. His grandmother would pick up a photograph, peer through her reading glasses with the crack in the right lens, would tap the image with her nail and whisper, "Now this is Papa."

The first photograph of his great-grandfather,

the earliest, was a mere four inches tall, what was called a *carte de visite*. If you stared long enough into its sepia depths, you could just make out the image of two little boys, solemn, with hair carefully parted, wearing shin-length trousers and roundabout jackets of identical cut but different size (as there was two years' difference in their age). One boy, James, sits on a deeply tufted, upholstered chair, luxuriant rope fringe cascading off the arm; the other, brother John, stands beside him. In marked contrast to the elegant furnishings and clothing, is the boys' feet, which are completely bare, without any sign of a shoe. This was Reconstruction North Carolina, after all. Shoes were thin on the ground in those exceedingly lean times.

There were other photographs was well. One showed James as a young man with a thick moustache, wool suit with waistcoat, and a smart, felt hat, the edges evenly turned up all around the circumference of the brim. He was newly married, according to family lore, to Frances, his second wife. Another image depicted a band of seated, jolly fellows, horizontally arranged like a Renaissance Last Supper, sitting in front of what looked to be a tent out in some woods. They were all holding enormous slices of watermelon, James included, and they, every one, seemed to be having a merry old time. Then there was a snapshot of James as an old man, walking in front of a huge, Civil War-era cannon that was dominating a village green. Curiously, as he appeared to be slackening away from the camera, the viewer is only presented with his black-hatted, retreating figure.

One photograph however, held a pre-eminent position amongst the lot. Will had been given it by the eldest daughter of the eldest of the sisters, those three orphaned daughters of James and Mary Jane. It was a tin-type and consisted of the image fixed onto a coated sheet of metal, roughly eight inches by ten inches, considered quite large for that particular type of photograph. It had attached to it by an ancient piece of string, an identical sized piece of colourless card, which acted as a sort of cover. Sometimes Will would hold this up to his nose, sniffing to detect if it's aroma would perhaps reveal any remnants of its past life with the sisters. The image, greenish-yellow and of an almost eerie clarity, was of a young man and a young woman, each leaning toward the other, elbows draped over a massive, turned pedestal squatting between them. They were James and his bride Mary Jane. They, obviously dressed in their best clothes, were in the flush of youth, and one could not help but wonder if this was not their wedding photograph.

Mary Jane was attired in an elaborately draped and layered dress, typical of the 1880's, and a plait of hair cascaded over her shoulder and down her breast. She looked every bit the fifteen year-old that she was. You could just make out in the young James's face, the ruddiness still in his cheeks, and the faintly dark area above his lip revealed that the razor did not frequent it very often. Through the thin fabric of his suit, you could make out the wiry, bony frame of a young man, long before the thickening and heaviness of middle age set in. His posture revealed itself to be full of energy, cocksure, as though he would spring out of the confines of the metal plate of the photograph at any given moment. He leaned jauntily, one elbow on the pedestal and one leg crossed in front of the other, the toe of his shoe balancing perfectly on point on the floor.

Even though you could just make out in the background the bracing apparatus used in those days to hold still the sitter's head for the long duration of the exposure, this photograph, unlike most that you see from this era, with the figures looking as wooden as the props they stand amongst, was almost arresting in its depiction of vigour. James's expression was nothing less than the embodiment of youthful exuberance and promise. Not only this, but he was, by anyone's standards, rather arresting in his beauty; it was this face that came to mind whenever Will thought of his great-grandfather.

As he went to close the box, he noticed the corner of a photograph sticking out of the stack diagonally. So that he could attempt to put things in order - a picture sticking out like that was liable to be damaged - he pulled it out of the stack. Taking a quick glance at it before he placed it safely back amongst the others, confirmed that it was an old snapshot of the very same James. Here he was outdoors, surrounded by what looked like a pair of boilers and other parts of a great steam engine. Standing on top of one of the huge boilers, looking into the camera, was a stout black man in a peaked cap. James, wearing a straw hat and clad in overalls, his watch chain draped across his chest, was bent over a low table, tools about him, apparently studying a set of plans. His moustache was long and white with age. *The Jack of all trades,* Will thought to himself. *He was the Jack of all trades.* If he were in any way uncertain if this were indeed his great-grandfather, Will had only to consult the recognisable hand-writing of his grandmother underneath the figure, spelling out, "Papa."

VIII

Slowly and absentmindedly he emptied moving boxes that day. Soon he forgot about Colin sitting there at the computer, not offering even so much as to make a cup of tea. After Will's initial irritation, he realised that it was better for him to do the unpacking anyway. Colin only got in the way, messed things up, and usually ended up breaking something. All the while, in the back of his mind was the cupboard, and what to do about it. Now and then he would open a box, the contents consisting of items that were normally housed in it: antique glass, crockery, etc., and they would remind him that they could not be put away. This would bring on another bout of panic and another round of deliberating over how he could get the cupboard into the flat. It wouldn't go into the lift; it wouldn't go up the stairs. He momentarily considered hoisting it up to the balcony, but dispensed with the idea almost immediately when he realised how many storeys they were above ground.

An idea, no matter how briefly, would pop into his head, to cut the feet off or some other drastic measure, and it would make him physically sick even picturing it. He pondered the nail holes that he had noticed along the top, the tale-tell signs that there had been something there, a moulding, crown, something that made the unfinished plank across the top more elegant. Someone had probably had the same problem before, had stumbled into a tight squeeze, and had removed it. Will would not have been the first to run into this catastrophe then, but this offered him no ease to his worrying. Someone may have been there before, but they could not offer any help or suggestion for him today, today in London, so far away. Still, the idea of somehow dismembering it stayed with him.

To his credit, he did at least know how this great hulk was constructed. The years of living with it, refinishing it, studying it had taught him that. His years of study of design and decorative arts had revealed to him that the cupboard belonged to category of furniture called Joinery, that is, it was a "joined" piece, meaning that its structure consisted basically of horizontal rails and vertical stiles. The rails and stiles were joined together, creating a rigid framework, and this framework was held together by delicate wooden pins. Filling the voids between the rails and stiles were the panels, which essentially floated in the voids, seated in grooves specially constructed for that purpose. It was a beautiful and time-tested system, Joinery. Unfortunately, Will was familiar enough with this complex and delicate wainscot-type construction to understand that it could not be taken apart without doing irreparable damage. He mulled over this for hour after hour, not seeing a way around it, until he felt completely enveloped in blackness.

Endlessly, he posed the question of how to make it shorter, how to make it narrower. He knew this was not possible, and it dogged him all afternoon, through cup after cup of tea. The piece of furniture was simply too tall and too wide. It could not snake around the obtuse, ridiculous turnings of this modern, pointless stairwell without running into them, snagging itself, until it could not move forward or backward. The photo that he had seen earlier kept hanging around in his thoughts as well. He could see his great-grandfather, the plans, the tools, flashing across his mind's eye. He could see the stout, black man, awaiting word to faithfully execute the plan. His grandfather could take apart a cotton gin and put it back together. He knew how to extract the oil from cottonseed. He had dodged the Spanish Flu and had survived the bonesetter. He had stared General Sherman in the face and lived to tell the tale. Will was certain that were he here, he could find a way. He could run right around it, or run smack into it, should he take the notion.

Slowly, by degrees, something did come to him. He remembered in the many times that he had moved house, that while the front and sides of the cupboard were indeed constructed in the intricate rail and stile mode, he recollected that the back of the piece consisted of extremely wide pine planks, simply but neatly nailed into the carcass. Maybe, he reasoned, just maybe if they could come off, then the whole bulk of it would in effect become hollowed out, and perhaps, just perhaps, if it were hollow, it could be conducted around those damned, infernal, concrete stair rails. Therefore, he would need to loosen the back boards until they could be removed. It was a radical idea, but he knew that it was probably the only one he had at the moment. He rehearsed the process several times in his head, refining it each time. This would not be easy he well knew, but at least the "dirty work" would take place on the back, on the rough, unfinished boards that were not seen and were never meant to be seen. Any damage he inflicted would be well and truly hidden.

Now that the idea had revealed itself, it would not let go of him. He could think of nothing else. The guilt that had so permeated his consciousness was now overlaid with the near manic repetition of his proposed, radical deconstruction of his heirloom. The idea streamed through his head, endlessly, like a tape loop. His mood brightened, only just, at the prospect of his coming up with a viable solution, but when he thought of actually carrying it out and all that it would entail, he reverted to his black nervousness. Wondering if he could wait until tomorrow, when he would be fresher, he weighed this against what he knew would be the almost unbearable nagging until morning. He wandered from room to room in the cluttered flat, dodging boxes and stacks of books, bedding, pots and pans, focussing on nothing, seeing nothing beyond the pictures reeling and spinning in his head.

Presently, he found himself in the kitchen, and without his even ruminating on the fact, he realised that he was focussing on his tool box, a sleek, enamelled metal casket, a gift from his father, from Sears & Roebuck. He walked over and knelt in front of it as he raised the hasp and lifted the lid. After studying the contents for a moment, he began removing tools one by one, screwdrivers, pliers, hand planes, and wrenches (which he knew the British called spanners). At last he came to a hammer, an old, rusty one with a smooth wooden handle. He inspected it for a moment and carefully laid it beside him. Then he pulled out a flat, metal tool, one end of which was turned at a ninety degree angle. This was what people called a "jimmy." He laid this beside the hammer and returned the other tools to the box one by one. He continued to kneel there in front of the toolbox for a few moments, lost in thought.

"What I need......What I need....I need," he said over and over as though he were repeating something from the rosary, and he climbed to his feet, clutching the hammer and the jimmy.

Then he began his search. He went from room to room, opening cupboards and doors, on a mission to find the thing that he could not articulate. He didn't know what it was he was looking for exactly, but he knew full well that he would recognise it when he saw it. In the foyer, he pulled open the door to the little airing cupboard with its shelves of wooden slats for towels and linen.

He stared at the shelf in front of him for a moment and said to himself, "Yes. That'll do"

At this, he took his hammer and hit one of the slats from underneath. It's right side immediately was raised a bit off of the support. He hit the left side in the same fashion and the wooden slat flew up into the air momentarily and hit the floor with a loud ping. Although completely oblivious to all the work that Will had been doing all morning and afternoon, this caused Colin to jump up from his seat and bound out into the foyer.

"What are you doing?" he said.

"Nothing," Will said. "I need this."

"So you're destroying the flat?"

"I'm not destroying the flat," Will shot back.

Colin could always get his dander up. He gathered up the slat, hammer, and jimmy, opened the door and stepped out on to the landing.

"I'm going over to work on this cupboard," he said.

"What are you going to do?"

"Nothing," Will said.

"Should I come with you?"

"No," Will said a little too quickly. Then softening a little, he added, "I'll be back."

"It's getting dark," Colin said.

Will looked through the metal grating on the landing which overlooked a flat roof littered with rotting carrier bags, take-away flyers, and mouldy rags. The sun was low on the horizon, promising dusk setting in within a few minutes. Colin was right. By the time he got into the van, he would have lost his light. He hung his head in frustration and huffed.

"I'll have to do it tomorrow," he said.

IX

From his earliest days, Will had been taught that the Crowells, his grandmother's family, breathed a different air than that of ordinary people. It was not that they were extraordinary in any way; it was more that their very living and breathing was somehow imbued with some vested quality that elevated them above the characterless. They were a tribe, so it appeared to Will, with flamboyant names and esoteric connections, associations which resulted in fantastic improbabilities, such as "double-half-cousins" and the curious circumstances that resulted in his own grandmother somehow being younger than her own niece.

He never forgot about the time that he had met the appropriately named Aunt Odd. She had been fetched from her home across town to be exhibited in his grandmother's front room one afternoon, and Will knowing that she was a direct, tangible link to the sisters and their mother Mary Jane, could remember looking on her, ancient and withered behind thick spectacles, and regarding her in the same way someone else might marvel at the presence of a shin bone or a mummified thumb encased in crystal.

When stories of the family were recounted, it wasn't the simple retelling of events. There was a gravity to them that made them more akin to the well-practiced stories he heard in Sunday School. They told about how James was a "Jack of all trades," and although Will, as a child had no idea what this meant, the very sound of it filled him with wonder and made him know that it was something rarefied. They told about how he could turn his hand to anything and had invented a process by which to extract the oil from cotton seed, only to be robbed by some unscrupulous scallywag stealing his idea and patenting it, leaving him with nothing.

They told about how he had lost his wife, leaving him with three small girls to raise, and they recalled how even in later years, when his own children would bring home a potential spouse for him to meet, he would ask, without hesitation, "Do you have any consumption in your family?" And they told how he married again, to the red-headed school teacher, his great-grandmother, who took on raising his three girls as her own, then went on to have four boys, and then an auburn-haired baby girl, his grandmother.

They told about how one of the boys, Will's great-uncle Guy returned home to Matthews in 1918 on leave from the army during the Great War, burning up with fever. Exhausted, he climbed into the bed with his younger brother Ted, not knowing that he had unwittingly come down with the Spanish flu. His great-grandmother, in response, boiled onions and made the entire family partake of the broth for days on end.

"The platform at Matthews train station was stacked high with coffins," his grandmother would tell, concerning their home town, "but we didn't lose a single one of our family; not one of us died of the Spanish flu."

His grandmother told of how her father James's work with the Lumas Ginning Company had required that he relocate for a time down to Columbus, Georgia. He travelled down there, ahead of his family, and found lodgings, a huge, rambling Victorian house with porches wrapping completely around it. He then wired the family to follow, which they did. Their journey was a long, dusty, tiring trip on the train, which landed them in Columbus late in the evening, exhausted and famished. There was no food in the house, but his great-grandmother managed to "scratch up" a meal somehow.

"We were starving to death," his grandmother would tell, "and all we had was some streaked meat. Mama fried that up, and I'll never forget as long as I live how good that streaked meat tasted. I Swanee, that was the best thing I believe I have ever eaten in my life."

They told how after the War, when James was approaching sixty years old, and his health was deteriorating, and not finding the visits from the doctor coming to anything, Will's great-grandmother Frances decided to consult a chiropractor, chiropractic in those days being seen as a panacea for general health disorders. His grandmother told the story that her father's screams of pain, as the chiropractor attempted to manipulate the old man's joints, could be heard all the way down Main Street in Matthews. The family was so traumatised that Frances vowed never to call upon the services of anything resembling a chiropractor again.

Of his death, on Christmas day - the doctors declared it "Oedema of the lungs" - Will could recall his grandmother speaking with hushed tones and profound sadness, as though it had occurred only recently. As he got older, Will was rather shocked when he realised that James had died all the way back in 1924 and not just a few years previously, such was the lingering profundity the family mourning.

Perhaps Will's favourite story, the one he most liked to hear, was the one about James's mother, Will's great-great grandmother, Jane Orr. It seems that at the height of the War Between the States, and with her husband John Monroe Crowell working away from home (he was in the sawmill business) Jane found herself in the unfortunate situation of staying with relatives who lived down in Camden, South Carolina. Hearing the ominous rumours about the impending approach of General Sherman and his bloodthirsty band moving northward from Savannah, she decided to make an attempt to flee the area, which was deemed to be in the army's path. Gathering up James, who was not yet three years old, and his younger brother, John, who had only been born a few months earlier, she high-tailed it in the direction of Charlotte, to the awaiting protection of the Orrs and the Alexanders, her people. Not realising, however, the extent of the assembled forces, nor their exact whereabouts, Jane miscalculated. Rather than dodging the oncoming marauders, like she intended, she somehow managed to wander right into their path, where she encountered the bellicose entirety of the Union forces, troops, artillery, the lot, including General William Tecumseh Sherman himself.

Will's great-grandmother would cackle with laughter, displaying the deep pink gums of her false teeth, when she recalled the tale.

"Instead of missing old Sherman like she intended," she would declare, "Grandmaw Jane ran smack INTO him."

At this she would clap her withered old hands together, and her watery-blue eyes would twinkle at the revelation. Although he was too young to have comprehended it at the time, James Ardrey Crowell had looked that cut throat General Sherman in the eye and had lived to tell the tale. It was a badge of honour that he would wear for the rest of his life, and even then some.

As the years wore on, and Will's great-grandmother entered her nineties, the spotlight was more and more on her. When she reached her one hundredth birthday, it became quite common for the local newspapers to publish articles about her.

They usually had headlines attached to them, such as "Still Knitting after 100 years," or "No Cigarettes or Alcohol for Centenarian." While the family were pleased with the attention, they were however not surprised at it. It only made sense that the wider world would come to recognise the esteemed life of this family. It was with some dismay to Will when he learned, a few years after the fact, that President Johnson actually sent a letter to every centenarian in the country, and not just to the one in his own family.

Will adored his great-grandmother, possibly because she doted on him and paid him all the attention that he craved, or possibly because that even at such a young age, he already knew that she was set apart, that she was endowed with something rich and almost miraculous. While his parents and grandparents spent an evening in the front room, seated around the folding card table, locked in a fiercely competitive and cut-throat game of Canasta, he would be in his great-grandmother's bedroom, watching her knit and tat. Although he was a typically rambunctious little boy, he was also dreamy, even melancholy. He would sit at her feet and quietly listen to her tell about the old days, when she was girl. She told of the tricks that she, her sisters, and her brothers used to play on each other: the girls short-sheeting the boys' beds in retaliation for the boys placing bushels of apples in the girls' bed. She described how she had attended a log schoolhouse, which had had the mud chinking between the logs removed, in order to admit more daylight, so that the students could better see their lessons. And she told about how she remembered those hard times when the hated Yankees still occupied North Carolina.

One of his earliest memories of her had proved to remain one of the most enduring. Once, when he was a small child, he was staying overnight at his grandparents. His great-grandmother's room contained twin beds, and into the empty bed was where his grandparents placed him for the night. His memory was that of his great-grandmother in the bed opposite, saying her prayers. The room was half lit by an old, plaster nightlight in the shape of a kitten chasing a ball of yarn, and he could remember watching the silhouette of the ancient woman's shadow on the wall opposite, rising and falling in time to the metre of her prayer, which she wheezed, "Our Father......Who art in Heaven....Hollowed be thy name..." He regarded her, when he came to think on it later, as he imagined the pious English must have regarded Good Queen Bess, when she still walked the earth, half Matriarch and half Madonna.

And so when she finally died at nearly one hundred and two years old, her passing was marked as the end of an era, with all the appropriate ceremony. Family converged from all over the country. The funeral home were forced to make special arrangements to contain the throngs of mourners arriving for the evening visitation, and the police were needed to escort the unusually long funeral cortege to the primordial Presbyterian burial plot. They made a visit to the old family home place, a modest dog trot log house located in the now dwindling countryside where she had been born and raised, where they tiptoed around the musty rooms, awed like pilgrims visiting an ossified cave. And afterwards, from there on out, the cupboard was to store yet another association. Whereas it had heretofore been an esteemed, sad, love-token, even an object of mystery and exoticism, it was now, in Will's eyes, a relic of his dear, hallowed great-grandmother as well.

X

Will was awake early the next morning, at first confused by the unfamiliar surroundings of the new flat. He looked out the window down to the concrete "public plaza" below with its broken benches and overturned bins. The distance of five stories could not improve it. His preoccupation with the plight of the cupboard from the day before continued throughout the night, ceasing only in the hiatus of his fitful sleep. Even his dreams were littered with it.

He could recall being in a room somewhere. It was a strange unknown place but at the same time familiar to him, and he was busily gathering things together for a move, things that turned out to be shoes, dozens and dozens of shoes.

His grandmother was there, somewhere, hovering there over him, and she said to him, "Now Sonny, don't forget, that's Papa."

There were stacks and stacks of shoes in the

room, and he was moving them one by one, attempting to keep them in order, attempting to find the mates. However, when he would turn around from moving a shoe, the stack would be different, having changed somehow, and he could not remember where he had stopped or from which stack he had taken the shoe, or where the mate that he had just seen now was. Each moment he stood there, he became more befuddled.

He could hear his grandmother, who presided over the growing mayhem saying in the background, "We didn't lose a single one."

Then, as he grew more and frustrated at his task, he could hear his her shouting from another room, some room nearby, "You've ruined it Sonny. You've ruined it."

He conducted an internal debate over what would be an appropriate time to go and knock on the brothers' door. By nine o'clock he was pacing the floor, but he knew that would be too early for them, they who had no doubt spent the previous evening at the seedy, working-class pub around the corner, called "The Surprise." Will had bravely stuck his head in the place one day and had concluded that the surprise was that you managed to come out alive. By ten he was practically climbing the walls, having emptied box after box, in an attempt to put his life back in order after the move, and as a means of filling in the gap of time until he could set out for his appointed task. Finally, at half-past ten, unable to wait any longer and unable to listen to another word of the inane television programme that Colin had been watching at full volume, he grabbed his tools and left the flat.

Within a few minutes, he arrived at the old estate. Already, it looked different to him, noticeably cleaner, more looked after, and somehow greener. He had never rated the unadorned, Depression-era, blocks before, but now he could not help but to suddenly find them charming with their tawny-coloured brick and their simple, municipal, Art Deco detailing. After repeated knocking, he managed to get the brothers' mother to the door, and then after several more minutes, one of the brothers himself, looking a bit sleepy, a bit drunk.

"Hey mate," the brother said, yawning and rubbing his eye.

"Do you think you could let me into the back of the van? I've got an idea about this cupboard," Will said.

The brother came back with a key, and they proceeded around the corner to where the van was parked at the far end of the estate. Will thought he would be asked what his plan was, but the brother remained silent. He couldn't tell whether he, the brother, had been sleeping or was just drunk, as he lazily released the lift platform and rolled up the shutter. There the cupboard was, just as it had been when Will had last seen it. It being in the empty van, looking abandoned, however, struck him somehow, and he was momentarily overcome with emotion, something akin to remorse. He struggled to keep from letting out a little cry.

He climbed up into the van and said to the brother, "I'm alright here on my own. You don't need to hang around if don't want to."

The brother looked relieved at this, saying, "OK mate, I'll leave you to it. Just lock it up when you're done."

He left without making any enquiry whatsoever as to what Will was intending to do.

Will watched his retreating figure and shook his head, muttering, "Jesus, somebody's had a good time."

He then turned his attention back to the cupboard standing there before him. With some effort, he slid one side of it out from the inside wall of the van, revealing the dark back. This was composed, just as he had remembered, of three very wide, vertical planks, which he could see were nailed at intervals into the carcass and the interior shelves. Over the years, with the slow drying of the timber, planks as wide as these had obviously shrunk across their width, which had created gaps between them. Someone - he wondered who - had stuffed long twists of cotton into the gaps, something to keep pests out he reasoned, when this piece of furniture still had a utilitarian function, that of storing food.

It was as he had supposed: the back boards were nailed, not pinned, albeit with stout, square nails, which meant that with some care and finesse, they could possibly be removed. Replaying the manoeuvres in his head for yet another time, he stood there, fixed, engrossed in thought. He opened the upper doors, revealing the red-painted interior, somewhat subdued in the half-light of the van. There on the bottom shelf, a length of old-fashioned, red and white check, oilcloth was affixed, just as it had been for as long as Will could remember. Then the smell came up and met him, embraced him like an old, dear friend, that comforting aroma of decaying oilcloth mixed with country ham. He paused at this, as though he were taking the time to exchange pleasantries with an old acquaintance. He knew, however, that he was stalling, putting off what he knew he had to do. He exhaled with such force that he could feel the wind of it on his arms and hands.

Armed with the hammer in one hand and the scrap of airing cupboard shelf in the other, he said to himself, "For what I have done...and for what I have failed to do."

He took the length of shelf wood, pushed it tight up against one of the backboards, from the inside, and whacked it with the hammer. The noise was like an explosion in the empty metal of the van, and although it was he himself who had caused it, it startled him nonetheless. He stretched his neck inside to see if there had been any movement. There was nothing, only the removal of a fleck of red paint, revealing a small white square. He repeated the process, but harder, and was greeted by the appearance of a space between the shelf and the backboard. He hit again, and the space opened a bit wider. He walked around to the back, took his block of wood and placed it above the nail hole and hit it.

Immediately, from out of the nail hole, he saw the head of an old-fashioned square nail.

He nailed that, Will thought to himself, *and nobody has disturbed it, until now.*

The green-yellow, tin-type visage of his forebear penetrated his mind's eye, much like the daylight that was just beginning to slip through the newly forced opening on the back of the cupboard. The image remained there whilst he secured the end of the nail in the hammer claw and pulled hard. There was a groan as the nail was pulled out, and the very sound of it made him sicken and close his eyes. For the life of him he could not help but think it sounded like a painful wail, surely loud enough to be heard all the way down the street. Uttering a small, private whimper, Will then took a deep breath, coughed, and carried on.

Within a few minutes, he was able to gently take his pry bar and pull the board from off of the back of the cupboard. On the one side, it was red with the intervening strips of unpainted wood where the shelves had intervened; on the other it was nearly black. He carefully laid this board on the floor beside him. He then came back around to the front to repeat the process of loosening the second board. He felt as though he were in some sort of a trance, or even that he was hovering some distance away, back and above, and was watching, not actually participating in what was going on.

He took his hammer and scrap of wood and hit the second board with same ferocity as he had hit the first one. Again, it was only after several blows was he able to prise the enormous plank, by degrees, from the carcass. He laid it beside the first one and turned to face the third board, the last one attached to the cupboard. Again, he moved around to the back and struck the board in several places, revealing the rectangular heads of the black, tapering nails. With the claw, he removed one, then another nail, each time the sickening groaning accosting his ears. He reached up with the hammer and grabbed one nail with the claw, high up at the top and pulled, but the nail did not budge. He changed his grip on the wooden handle and pulled again, but the nail did not move. He changed his grip again and pulled down with great force, gritting his teeth.

In a split second, he was faintly aware of some sudden movement, then a great crack of energy, and then he saw white. It was white with a spreading filament like the bulb of a night light. He heard the hammer drop onto the floor and he was aware that something, he, was reeling backwards. There was a swirl, black, and red, and veiny. Another second and he could sense that he was now doubled over frontwards. There was a groaning, which at first he attributed to the pulling out of the nails embedded in the hard, heart pine, but then it sunk in that he was the one emitting it.

A sharp pain shot through his head like electric sparks, and he was vaguely cognisant of the fact that both of his hands were pressed tightly to his forehead.

"Mother of God," he moaned in anguish.

He became aware of an even, pulsing cadence coursing through him, like the slow, measured verses of a well-rehearsed orison being recited, line after line. He could see a silhouette, rising and falling in the distance in time with this surging, pulsing cadence. There was a kitten, with a grimacing, painted face, its paw on a faintly pink-rendered ball, illuminated by a pulsing, thunder-veined bulb.

This was only interrupted by another sensation, a heavy, sticky warmth coating his fingers and palms, issuing forth, keeping time with the pulsing. At this, he was urged to open his eyes. In his distorted, swirling vision he saw redness, the dripping, dropping redness of his own blood splattering onto the dark, rough surface of the cupboard plank lying on the floor. The even metre of the pulse melded into and transformed into an overwhelming throbbing in his temple and forehead. A wave of nausea came over him and he slowly lowered himself to the floor, reaching out a bloody hand onto the backboard beside him to steady himself as he clumsily descended. He hit the floor with a thud and sat there a few seconds breathing heavily.

Once seated for he few minutes, his legs sprawled in on direction, his arms in the other, he lifted his hand and saw a sticky red hand print on the black of the wood. He sat there in a stupor. Out of the corner of his eye, he saw the hammer on the floor with the nail, the reluctant nail, still wedged into the claw.

"I guess I got it pulled out then?" he said to himself.

Turning back to the plank on the floor, he noticed the handprint again. It was already diminished in its intensity, the bright, livid ruddiness of just a few moments before seeming to be rapidly seeping into the dry, old wood.

"Hell's bells," he said by way of exclamation.

Indeed, the blood drops and splatters that had fallen onto the plank were rapidly being incorporated into the darkness. In contrast, the blood that was on the floor of the van was still bright red and liquid. Momentarily, he gathered his courage and placed a tentative finger on his forehead. It was unfamiliar and not quite recognisable with its swelling and the gash that was still pumping out blood.

"Damn," he said, "bleeding like a stuck pig."

Deciding that he had better not attempt to stand just yet, he closed his eyes, trying to overcome the waves of nausea and throbbing pain.

"Guess I'll live," he said, deciding to try to make the best of it.

He didn't know whether a minute or maybe ten minutes had passed, the pounding in his head powerful and loud, but he decided to make an effort to stand. Rolling himself over onto his knees, he reached for the now fully-exposed bottom shelf of the cupboard to hold on to. Reaching for each successive shelf, he managed to pull himself up to a standing position. Once upright, he came to realise that he was positioned at the back of the cupboard, now completely robbed of its backboards, as though he were inside, placed in the vantage point of looking out through the open doors. The shelves were there before him, almost like wooden caskets one atop the other, and the effect was something akin to looking down the wrong end of a pair of binoculars.

Here like a country ham, he thought to himself, only to blush for thinking something so silly.

"I must have knocked myself winding," he said.

As he stood there, still a bit shaky, and bit woozy, his gaze was drawn to something small and rectangular stuck to the back of the shelf right before him. It was a small shred of thin parchment, and Will realised that it had only just been exposed by the removal of the backboards, having apparently slipped in between them and the shelf at some time in the past. He peeled it away and held it up, straining to focus, what with the pounding in his head. It was a fragment, looking to be accidentally torn from a book or tract; he could just make out the following:

> *...solemn occasion; but occasionally devout pilgrims who have come there merely for that purpose beg that it be shown them as a reward for their long journeying. It is said that ..... gift alone that these tiny fragments of sacred wood from the......*

He couldn't make heads or tails of the fragment, and it was only after he had read the inscription, that he realised he had smeared blood on it. He stared at it a moment longer, and rather absentmindedly stuffed it into the pocket of his jeans. It was only now that he was beginning to come to a realisation of what he had just carried out, the sheer violence of the act momentarily overshadowing the denouement. It appeared that he had done what he had set out to do, the transformation having been carried out. The cupboard, from his point of view, was practically unrecognisable. It was hollowed out, like a mummified, uncorrupted body. It was dismembered, the parts seemingly bound for display, like a shin bone or a dried thumb, behind a distant, crystal dome. For the time being, Will had done all that he could be expected to do.

The throbbing in his head was joining up with a truly sharp headache by this time, and he was feeling more than a bit sick. Tapping one of the shelves with his forefinger, he wheeled about and picked up the widest of the backboards, walking it over to the lift of the removals van. He unsteadily lowered himself down to ground level and pulled the shutter down. Then, adjusting the heavy pine plank as best he could for balance, he set off for the new estate. A woman with shopping bags crossed to the other side of the street when she caught sight of him. The rough edge of the board bit into his hand as he eased the door open to the staircase at the tower block, where he was met with the familiar smell of dust, cheap detergent, and old piss.

Readjusting the cumbersome piece of wood, he started the ascent, upward, around what seemed endless twists and turns, each one bringing on a new layer of dizziness. His breathing began to match in pace the throbbing in his head, as he passed the spot where not twenty-four hours before they all stood, stuck, unable to pass. Only after what seemed like an interminable fumble with the keys did he get the door to the flat open and the plank inside. He closed it abruptly on the pudgy neighbour boy, the bicycle thief, who had been standing out on the landing, gawping.

Colin walked in from the other room, took one look, and let out a gasp.

"What happened?" he shouted.

"Rather than missing him, I ran smack into him," Will said.

"Ran into who? Who did you run into?" Colin demanded.

"No one, a hammer. I had a little accident."

"Are you bleeding?"

"I'm fine. A head this hard won't break," Will said, attempting some humour.

"What's that? Is that from your cupboard? Colin asked, pointing to the plank.

Will shot him a look.

"Did you destroy it?" Colin continued.

"Why Sonny, you've ruined it," Will squealed, mimicking the drawl of an old Southern woman.

Not understanding any of this whatsoever, but getting the distinct impression that he was being mocked, Colin, in a mild huff, went back into the bedroom and to his game, grumbling, "You need to have that bump looked at.....bastard."

"Why shut my mouth General Sherman," Will called out, "I do declare, you just say the nicest things."

Realising that he was now alone in the entry hall, he trailed off, "And all we had was the streaked meat, Mama."

XI

The next day, they were there, the three of them, standing in the back of the removals van, the two brothers and Will. The brothers were marvelling at Will's handiwork, not to mention the dried remains of blood on the floor.

"Mate, I can't believe you smacked yourself in the 'ead," one of them said, leaning over and scrutinising the shell-shaped abrasion on Will's forehead.

Will just shook his head, which the brother took to mean that he agreed.

"And how did you get it apart? I mean, how did you even fink of it?" the other brother asked.

"Well, I had a pretty good notion of how my granddaddy built the thing. So, that was a start I guess," he said.

Then casting a glance over toward the cupboard, he added, "Of course knowing a thing and then being able to carry it out, well that's a horse of different colour entirely…..very different colour entirely, as I have found out to my detriment."

He guffawed at this last bit, gingerly touching the shell-shaped abrasion.

"Well done mate," the first brother said.

"I didn't have any choice," Will said, "Besides, you don't think I was going to leave it down here for you two tow rags to go sell up North End Road do you?"

The two brothers looked at each other, not knowing if they had been insulted or not, and there was an awkward moment's silence, but then one of them burst into laughter, followed by the other.

"Nice one mate, yeah," they said, slapping him on the back. "Yeah, nice one."

"You reckon we can shift it up that stairwell now?" the one brother asked.

"Yeah, it'll go up there now I believe," Will said, attempting to sound confident. "If it doesn't, I'll just have to hit myself in the head until it does," he added. "I carried the biggest of the those backboards up yesterday, and it made it without a problem. So, that's something I suppose."

"With your head bleeding and all? Damn mate, respect," the brother said.

Will gazed down at the blood on the floor, dried red-brown like wood stain, and the two remaining backboards, the blood spots now practically invisible, having been incorporated into the dark, old pine.

"It wasn't so bad," he said. "I just picked it up and carried it off. That's what you do."

Will scrutinised the cupboard standing before him, hollowed out, deconstructed, and hardly recognisable. It was a disquieting sight, like encountering the handiwork of a solemn, purposeful disinterment. It was going to take a bit a work to put it all back together, but he would deal with that in time. Perhaps it was the residual effects of the blow to the head, but he was sensing, somewhere in his waters, the violent recognition of a sort of illuminated resignation deep within him. He was not the first, and may not even be the last; he was just the latest. This is how it had come to this. It was not remarkable; it was simply the way things were. He never questioned, not one jot, not one tittle, of why it was he, why he was that one, the latest, any more than he questioned the veracity of an aged, canonical, family story. Indeed, the thought had never entered his head.

He walked over and closed the doors, one at a time, preparing the cupboard for its journey up the stairs.

"We're an odd lot," he said, "We just pick it up and carry it on."

He turned his attention to the little propeller-shaped keep, where he latched the doors in place.

"And the funny thing is," he said, "sometimes we miss it, and sometimes we run smack into it."

Comprehending none of what Will had said – it was just the sort of gibberish that they had come to expect from him – the brothers, now fortified nonetheless, commenced, bowing to the appointed task set before them.

ABOUT THE AUTHOR

Jeffrey T Kiser-Paradi was born in Charlotte, North Carolina, where he was fortunate to come of age among the fallow cotton fields and falling-down barns of his grandparents' farm in rural Mecklenburg County. His fascination with history, antiques, genealogy, and the past in general, showed up early and inexplicably in his life, with his parents being rather stumped as to where the interest came from. He lived in Greensboro, North Carolina and New York City before moving to London in 1998, where he makes his home with Tibor, his husband of nine years.

He still longs for livermush.

19915494R00151

Printed in Great Britain
by Amazon